A
HOMEMADE
CHRISTMAS

OTHER BOOKS AND AUDIO BOOKS
BY ALMA J. YATES:

Race to Eden

Sammy's Song

A HOMEMADE CHRISTMAS

A Novel

Alma J. Yates

Covenant Communications, Inc.

Cover image © Eric Dowdle.

Cover design copyrighted 2007 by Covenant Communications, Inc.

Published by Covenant Communications, Inc.
American Fork, Utah

Printed in Canada
First Printing: October 2007

13 12 11 10 09 08 07   10 9 8 7 6 5 4 3 2 1

ISBN 978-1-59811-094-4

To my wife Nicki, who has always
exemplified the "giving thing."

CHAPTER 1

"This is it?" I gasped in open-mouthed, wide-eyed horror as we entered Eagar, Arizona, for the first time in late '74. "But there's nothing here, and it's so . . ." I groped for the right word and grimaced. "So ugly," I practically whimpered. "Dad said it'd be beautiful," I complained to my mother, who drove our loaded-down station wagon behind Dad in the U-Haul truck.

"It's not . . . so bad, Nadine," Mom responded slowly. Even though I was only eleven, I easily detected the uncertainty in her voice.

Eagar certainly didn't measure up to the elaborate fantasy I had naively conjured up in my mind after Dad announced we were moving to the White Mountains of Arizona. Foolishly, I had imagined a bustling hamlet nestled quaintly in pine- and aspen-covered mountains, their majestic peaks capped with brilliant snow.

By heartbreaking contrast, Eagar and her twin sister Springerville were two tiny communities in the middle of bleak hills and flatlands covered with dry, tarnished yellow-and-brown grass and littered with piles of black volcanic rock. When we first entered Eagar, it was early November, and the town's trees were nothing but dreary gray skeletons, stripped bare by fall frosts. There were no snow-capped, craggy peaks surrounding the town, and the pine- and aspen-covered mountains Dad had assured us existed were fifteen long miles away.

"But I thought it was going to be . . ." I choked back a cry, recalling my elaborate visions of green mountain meadows, deep-blue lakes, and meandering brooks.

Things got worse after we found our tiny, temporary home and began unloading our things. I cringed in the shadow of our U-Haul truck, surrounded by piles of bulging boxes and bags, sundry chairs, empty dressers, bulky mattresses, and box springs, all of which had to be crammed into our modest, three-bedroom rental house. The task appeared daunting, if not futile.

"It's not such a small house," Mom declared as all of us children moaned a protest, mine the loudest of all. I refused to believe that there was even the slightest ray of hope in our dreary circumstances. "Let's get things inside," Mom challenged cheerily. "We don't want to be working in the dark."

None of us kids had wanted to move to Eagar. Poverty had banished us there. And yet, we hadn't always been poor. Until a year earlier, Dad had owned and operated his own insulation business in Logan, Utah, where we had a decent home and most of what we needed. Unfortunately, our family's simple prosperity came to a screeching halt Thanksgiving Day when Dad retrieved my Frisbee from the roof of our house and slipped and fell headfirst onto the concrete driveway, giving himself a concussion, breaking both his arms and his hip, and puncturing his left lung.

Our whole world seemed to crash and crumble that day. Obviously Thanksgiving was ruined, and Christmas ended up being a shameful disaster as our family elicited unwanted pity and became the focus of several secret charity projects. I had been sure that I would expire from abject embarrassment.

Mom tried to keep the family business afloat, but with Dad unable to work and an avalanche of medical and business bills to pay, including a second mortgage on our home, there was little she could do to stave off financial disaster. Subsequently, we slipped from the security of the middle class into the humiliating depths of poverty. It was a new and frightening world, one that I loathed from the very beginning.

Five months after Dad's accident, our financial circumstances were complicated further when my oldest sister Tammy received a mission call to Denmark. I couldn't understand why God would strap one more burden on our poor family, but Mom optimistically predicted that blessings would pour from heaven if Tammy went. Sadly, Mom's promised blessings turned out to be my three uncles volunteering to pay for Tammy's mission, which did nothing for the rest of our family, except make me feel that we were indeed a genuine charity case.

I remember only too well our giant yard sale a few weeks before our move to Arizona. My best friend, Karen Abbott, simply couldn't believe that we were actually selling all our nice things. I was too embarrassed to admit the truth, so I lied guiltily, telling her that our plan was to get *better* things. I knew I'd be rescued from this fabrication because Evan Slade, one of Dad's former missionary companions who'd learned of our plight, had already invited Dad to take a job in Eagar as the foreman and head mechanic of Slade Sand and Gravel Construction.

And now I stood on the front lawn of our new home, surrounded by our shabby possessions. I'm not quite sure why I decided to open the old, green battered trunk. Perhaps in my melancholy mood I was searching for something to cheer me up. Unsnapping the silver clasps, I pushed up the lid and stared down at the family's neatly packed holiday decorations— strings of Christmas lights, boxes of tree ornaments, a ceramic nativity scene, and eight large Christmas stockings, one for each of us.

ALMA J. YATES

"Nadine, there's no sense opening the Christmas trunk," my sister Wendy remarked as she brushed past me. Wendy, a high school sophomore who had forfeited her spot on Logan High's spirit line to travel to Arizona, was in a bit of a foul mood. "Christmas is weeks away," she sneered.

"And that's not the worst of it," my seventeen-year-old brother Rusty injected heartlessly, hefting the coffee table and moving toward the house. "Christmas will skip all of us this year," he observed, glowering at our new home. Deep into sports at Logan High, Rusty had complained long and loud at the prospect of moving to Eagar. He was convinced that he was destined to either be the next Joe Namath for the New York Jets or follow JoJo White as Rookie of the Year and play for the Boston Celtics. Unfortunately, he was just as certain that no one would notice his fabulous potential in a remote corner of Arizona. Feeling the nasty bite of disappointment, he wanted me to feel it too. "You might as well pack that old trunk away," he growled. "It won't do us any good this year."

"We'll at least hang up our stockings," I returned hopefully. I no longer believed in Santa, but I clung desperately to the hope of a tiny miracle. "Maybe there won't be any *big* gifts, but there'll be *something* in our stockings."

Wendy and Rusty laughed cynically. "If there is," Wendy murmured, "it'll be a piece of last year's stale candy that got stuck in the toe." She suddenly squinted as though deep in thought. "Come to think of it, we didn't get any candy last year, so don't count on the stale candy either."

"Christmas will still come!" I declared defiantly, gritting my teeth.

"Is Nadine bawling *again*?" My brother Garrett mimicked a whimper and then flashed a mischievous grin. Only fourteen months older than me, Garrett was a relentless, mean-spirited tease.

"I wasn't bawling," I snapped, hurling a plastic bag full of clothes in his direction. He dodged it and laughed. I didn't want to believe Rusty's and Wendy's dire holiday predictions, but I was old enough to realize that currently we were little more than poor Mormons who'd been on the brink of hauling out our ominous food storage to feast on cracked-wheat mush and watered-down powdered milk.

I slammed the Christmas chest shut and fastened the silver snaps. Ruefully I picked up a cardboard box and lugged it toward the house, sniffling softly. Just before tromping up the front steps, I glanced toward the street and spotted a girl staring curiously. I had no idea how long she'd been there or what possible business she had loitering in front of our house. Quickly I looked away and charged up the steps, colliding with my oldest brother, Daniel. The box I was carrying bounced from my arms and tumbled down the steps.

"Whoa!" Daniel joked, steadying me. "We don't have to get everything in the house in one wild charge." He tugged playfully on my long hair before scooping up my box and placing it back in my arms. Without question, he was my favorite sibling. Unfortunately, in the middle of January he was abandoning us to go on a mission to Argentina. "Save some work for the rest of us," he added.

I cast a quick glance toward the girl in the street. She snickered and shook her head in obvious amusement. Fuming silently, I stomped into the house.

After depositing the box in the kitchen, I darted into the hall bathroom and regarded my reflection in the mirror. I brushed my shoulder-length, light brown hair from my eyes. Hurriedly I splashed water on my face and dabbed it off with a hand towel. Gulping, I forced myself to smile in the mirror. It was a fake, anemic smile, but it was enough to disguise my recent tears.

Before returning to our moving mess outside, I peeked out the window toward the street. Thankfully the girl was gone, so I ambled slowly out the front door and wandered among the boxes piled haphazardly on the front lawn.

"Are you just moving in?"

I screeched and whipped around clumsily, practically stumbling over a box packed with blankets. The girl sat soberly on a kitchen chair at the corner of the house.

Her arms were folded and her legs were propped up on a bulging box. "You're kinda jumpy," she observed with a wry smile.

"Where'd you come from?" I sputtered, glancing toward the street and half pointing in that direction as though indicating that was where she was supposed to be. "And I didn't jump," I insisted with an edge to my voice. "There are so many boxes around here you can't walk anyplace without tripping." I gritted my teeth. "And why'd you jump out at me like that?" I accused.

"I didn't jump anywhere. I was just sitting here. If I'd wanted to scare you . . ."

"You didn't scare me," I cut her off. "And you're sitting on our kitchen chair."

The girl unfolded her arms and stood up. "I didn't know it was a special chair. It looks pretty ordinary to me. Where you from?"

I studied the girl critically. She was small, almost five inches shorter than me, but she possessed a certain manner that hinted she was older than she looked. She had a mop of frizzy, reddish-brown hair. Her skin was light, almost pale, and her nose and cheeks were generously sprinkled with freckles. As she studied our possessions, she scrunched up her nose and pressed her lips together, and a deep dimple formed in her right cheek.

"We just moved here from Logan, Utah," I replied suspiciously, positive that this presumptuous girl didn't have a clue where Logan was, which was fine with me because I didn't want anybody in Eagar knowing of our embarrassing descent into poverty.

The girl picked up a paper sack stuffed with my clothes, looked inside uninterestedly, and then dropped the sack on the ground and moved on. "My Uncle Orson lived in Logan. We used to visit him there. His house was just down the hill from the temple. He worked at the college. He's dead now."

I glared at the girl snooping casually through our things. Her half-zipped sweatshirt revealed a splotch of mustard on the ragged T-shirt underneath, and her faded denim jeans had frayed cuffs and holes in both knees. She wore scuffed, dirty white tennis shoes with no socks, and her big toe peeked out from a hole in the left shoe. I scowled distastefully. This girl looked like an escapee from the local orphanage wandering a path of poverty more pronounced than my own. Secretly I hoped that all the kids in Eagar were as hard up as this girl; then my own poverty would seem normal.

"Why'd you move to Eagar?" the girl asked. "Not many people come here."

"My dad got a really good job," I bragged, assuming that if this girl even knew who her dad was, he was probably a drunk or a bona fide bum.

"A really good job?" she asked dubiously, scrunching up her nose and cocking her head to one side. "In Eagar? I didn't think Eagar had such a thing."

"He's going to be a foreman," I boasted, bristling.

"Who in Eagar needs a foreman?" the girl questioned smirkingly.

"Evan Slade. He owns a sand and gravel business."

"If your dad's the foreman," the girl grunted, "what's Evan going to do?" She didn't wait for an answer. "My name's Jennilynn Lewis, Jen or Squirt for short."

"Squirt?" I questioned, raising my brow.

"I'm kinda small, but I turn twelve in February." She shrugged. "Mom figures I'll hit a growth spurt one of these days. I hope so. I get tired of looking people in the belly button." Her gaze settled on our house. "How'd you end up with this place?"

"What's wrong with it?" I challenged. "I like it fine."

"Nothing's wrong with the place, just the duchess that owns it."

"The duchess?"

Jennilynn pointed to a huge two-story house set back from the street in a stand of bare-branch, white-bark aspen trees and towering ponderosa pines. I had been so caught up in the drama of seeing our new home that I hadn't paid much attention to anything in the vicinity. Now I studied the house immediately across the street, a large brick house surrounded by an incredibly spacious yard. The splendor was enclosed within brick pillars and black decorative wrought iron. The front of the house had three gabled second-story windows. Jennilynn pointed out that the massive front door was made of hand-carved oak and decorated with a brass knocker. If that weren't enough, it sported a stained-glass oval window. She also explained that in back was a full balcony overlooking a patio. There was a huge rock chimney on one end of the house that Jennilynn claimed went to a fabulously elaborate fireplace.

"Do you want to know what's really sickening about that house?" Jennilynn asked wryly. "It isn't her real house. Dad calls it her mountain cabin." Jennilynn shook her head. "Some cabin. Her real house is in Scottsdale."

I stared openmouthed and listened to Jennilynn. "I think your place was supposed to be the guest house or the servants' quarters or something, but you're the first ones to actually live here." Jennilynn hesitated. "You're not related to Mrs. Thurman, are you?" I closed my mouth and wagged my head. "I didn't figure her relatives would have your kind of stuff." Jennilynn's bluntness offended me, and I wanted to retaliate, but intuitively I knew that she was merely making an observation, not attempting to denigrate our family.

"What's she like?" I asked curiously. "Is she a real duchess?"

"Mainly she's just weird. She stays boxed up in that big house and hardly ever talks to anyone. That's fine because I doubt anybody wants to talk to her either."

"Hey, Nadine," Garrett growled at me, "there's still work to do."

"I'm leaving," Jennilynn said, holding up her hands. "Sometime I'll show you the town, not that there's much to see." She paused. "You've got a name, don't you?"

"Nadine. Nadine Cluff."

Jennilynn considered my name. "That's different. Not weird different. Just different. See you tomorrow, Nadine."

CHAPTER 2

The rest of the afternoon I cast curious glances toward the big house across the street and concocted imaginary tales about the mysterious duchess living there. I wondered if one day I'd spot a supermarket tabloid with the screaming headline "DUCHESS FORFEITS TITLE! LEADS SECRET LIFE IN EAGAR, ARIZONA."

Eventually I crept across the street and hid behind a clump of shrubbery for a better view. Furtively I studied every window, hoping to catch a glimpse of the enigmatic lady inside, but the drapes and blinds were closed.

Suddenly, one of the two garage doors opened, revealing the bright taillights of a white Cadillac El Dorado. Quickly I hunkered behind the shrubbery until the car moved slowly down the cement driveway and disappeared. In my anxiety, I didn't get even a peek at the duchess.

"Are we renting this place from the rich lady across the street?" I asked Dad that night as he put my bed together.

Dad dropped the box springs into place, straightened up, and ran his fingers through his thick, sandy brown hair. Lately it had become peppered with gray. "Evan said it was a widow living across from us." He frowned. "It's probably her."

My imagination exploded into wild possibilities. If Mrs. Thurman really was a rich duchess in seclusion, perhaps she'd take pity on our poor family. I smiled to myself, wondering if perhaps the duchess was God's way of showering us with the rich blessings Mom had talked about when Tammy had accepted her mission call.

"You ready for the big town tour?" Jennilynn called to me the next day as I came out the front door, my arms loaded with empty boxes. Jennilynn wore a yellow, buttoned blouse and a different pair of denim jeans, this pair old and faded too, but without the holes in the knees. She had on her same sweatshirt and ragged tennis shoes.

"I still have a few chores," I explained, stacking the boxes in our small garage, "but tell me more about the duchess."

"What's to tell?" She scratched her head. "And I didn't *exactly* say she's a duchess. Some of us call her that, but she's probably nothing but a rude, rich old lady."

"I almost saw her yesterday," I offered excitedly. "But I didn't get a good look because I was hiding in the bushes when she drove off. Where do you think she went?"

Jennilynn shrugged and looked askance at me. "Who knows? She does most of her shopping in Show Low and Phoenix." Jennilynn snickered and rolled her eyes. "Once I saw her out walking in a mink coat." She shook her head. "Normal people wear sweats, but the duchess breaks out a mink coat. Now that's weird!"

"She must be real rich to have a mink coat."

"She's got to be real something," Jennilynn said drolly.

"Does she have servants?"

Jennilynn pulled the corners of her mouth down. "Not servants like butlers and maids, but she hires out things. In the summer a gardener drives from Show Low three times a week to take care of her yard. Carmelita Baca does her cleaning and laundry and fixes her meals. Once she hired a guy to oil her front-door hinges." Jennilynn shrugged. "When you're done here, I'll give the tour. I live two blocks down, the second house from the corner on the left side, number 237. There are a couple of big pines in front."

After Jennilynn left, I was finishing up the last of my chores when I saw the white El Dorado back out of Mrs. Thurman's garage. More on wild impulse than actual plan, I snatched my beat-up bike from the garage and charged down the street in the direction Mrs. Thurman had gone the previous day. I was already pedaling furiously when her car passed me, but I figured that with a head start, I might be able to follow her.

The car turned three blocks ahead. By the time I reached the intersection, Mrs. Thurman's car was nowhere in sight, but the road she had taken led westward toward an arched gateway. I reached the gateway out of breath, and although it was a cool fall day, drops of sweat trickled down the sides of my face. Exhausted, I stared at the scene before me—the town cemetery.

The cemetery was laid out on a slope rising gently away from me. There was row after row of uniquely shaped headstones, some polished granite, others rough sandstone. A few of them were adorned with faded plastic flowers in glass jars. Yellowish-brown grass and weeds covered the ground. The place was quiet and appeared deserted; then I spotted Mrs. Thurman's Cadillac in the far corner.

Laying my bike down, I crept secretly from headstone to headstone, hoping to spy without being seen. When I was about fifty feet from the Cadillac, I dropped behind a three-foot square of gray granite and peered surreptitiously around its corner.

The car door slowly opened and a tall, imposing figure emerged. She was dressed in black—a calf-length skirt, a black sweater, a small black hat, and black gloves. Mrs. Thurman's black attire and black hair contrasted starkly with her pale face. She walked to the rear of the car, opened the trunk, and peered inside. After a moment of silent perusal, she removed a watering can and two five-gallon white plastic buckets, each covered with a blue lid. Straining and staggering, she lifted each separately from the car. Methodically she removed the lids and sloshed water into the watering can. When the can was filled, she took it to the front of the car, which was parked by a white marble headstone, larger than any other. Immediately in front of the headstone and surrounded by a black wrought-iron two-foot-high fence was a small plot of grass, ten feet by ten feet. The grass inside the enclosure, although not green and lush, was greener than anything else in the cemetery.

Mrs. Thurman opened a small gate in the wrought-iron fence, and starting in one corner of the tiny plot, began sprinkling the lawn by hand. She made several trips to the buckets until they were both empty. Then, replacing the buckets and watering can in the back of the car, she extracted a pair of shears, returned to the tiny plot, got down on her hands and knees, and proceeded to trim the grass by hand. All of her actions seemed rehearsed as though she were in a deep trance.

When the trimming was complete, she sat next to the white marble headstone, her head bowed, her gloved hands clasped in her lap—a plaintive picture of sorrow and longing. For a long time, her lips moved as though she spoke to someone.

I lay quietly, the dry yellow grass prickling my stomach, arms, and elbows while I watched. Eventually I backed away from my hiding place and crept back to my bike, my mind bursting with questions.

Forgetting my remaining chores, I charged straight for Jennilynn's house. The way she dressed I expected to find her living in a tumble-down, one-room shack with an invalid father and a sick, struggling mother. Precisely for that reason I was shocked when I saw the number 237 on the front of a very large, beautiful split-level home with two prominent ponderosa pines in front. As I gaped in wonder, still straddling my bike, the front door flew open and Jennilynn poked her red, frizzy head out and shouted, "Don't just gawk, come in."

Tentatively I stepped into Jennilynn's elegant home. The shag carpet and furniture were new. Everything was immaculate and orderly. The place was quiet except for the faintest strains of music coming from one of the rooms.

"This is where you live?" I gulped, feeling self-conscious and out of place.

"This is it. Do you want something to eat before we go?"

I looked around, a bit in awe. "Does anybody else live here?"

"No, I'm an orphan, so I've got the whole place to myself," Jennilynn joked, giving me a playful shove.

"Actually, Mom and Dad come home sometimes," she added with a grin, scratching her stomach. "Dad owns the grocery and variety stores here in town, so Mom and him are usually there. Hey, I'll show you my bedroom. I even cleaned it. But don't peek under the bed or in the closet. Not even Mom dares do that."

I was shocked to see that most everything in Jennilynn's bedroom was a soft, light pink. An enormous canopied bed covered with a thick, fluffy comforter took up a sizable chunk of the room. Two gigantic pillows were propped at the head of the bed, and a huge stuffed white bear lay between them. The mirrored dresser, the lamps and lamp tables, the desk and chair were all white with gold trim.

"Sorry about all the pink," Jennilynn grumbled. "I wanted bright red or dark blue, but Mom thinks pink might make a lady out of me." She shook her head and grinned.

Jennilynn gave me a quick tour of her house and then took me to the kitchen for Oreo cookies and milk. "I followed the duchess today," I reported, milk dripping from my cookie. I related what had happened when she looked interested. "What do you figure?"

Jennilynn pushed a milk-soaked cookie into her mouth and spoke while she chewed. "That's where Willard's buried. Or what's left of him."

"Who's Willard and what do you mean by 'what's left of him'?"

"Her husband. She cremated him."

"You mean, like, burned him up?" I choked.

"It's not like she had a weenie roast. She didn't bake him in her own oven."

I scowled. "You're kidding me, aren't you?"

Jennilynn held up her hands. "People get cremated all the time. That's what Willard wanted. He wrote it in his will."

I grimaced. "Normal people don't do junk like that."

Jennilynn laughed. "Who said Marge Thurman's normal? Besides, Willard's the one that told her what to do. You see, he started coming up here a long time ago to hunt and fish and camp and ski. Marge hardly ever came. A few years ago, he built the house you're in so Marge would have a place to stay." Jennilynn shook her head. "But she didn't like that little place. So Willard built the big house. She didn't really like that either. Actually, she just didn't like living up here. She figured she was too good for everybody." Jennilynn sighed. "Willard told Marge that when he died, he wanted her to scatter his ashes in all his favorite places so he'd be part of the country up here."

"Scatter his ashes? That's gross!" I thought a moment and then asked, "Hey, if Willard's ashes got scattered, why the big gravestone in the cemetery?"

Jennilynn scrunched up her nose and raked her fingers through her frizzy hair. "Marge didn't do *exactly* what Willard asked her to do. She kept some of his ashes in a little vase, locked the vase in an iron box, and buried it in the cemetery. Then she ordered that big headstone, planted grass all around it, threw up the iron fence, and made a regular little park right in the middle of the graveyard. I think that's the reason she won't go back to her big house in Scottsdale—she doesn't want to leave Willard."

I whistled softly. "That's just too weird. Why didn't she just put the ashes in a jar and keep it in her kitchen cupboard? Then she could talk to Willard there in her house."

"I didn't say anything about her talking to the ashes."

"She talks to somebody. If you don't believe me, come with me," I invited.

Jennilynn shook her head. "Mom doesn't like me spying on people." She dug a finger into her ear. "Do you know what's kind of spooky?" She stood, put the carton of milk in the fridge, and stuck the cookies in the cupboard. "Willard finished their house a year ago last summer. Just before Christmas he put up lots of lights and decorated the place like no other house in town. When everything was fixed just the way he wanted it, he had himself a big heart attack and died."

"At Christmastime?" I questioned, stunned.

"Isn't that a bummer of a time to die? Shoot, I'd hate to die at Christmastime. Christmas is my favorite time of year. How about you?"

Suddenly I became quiet, thinking about last Christmas, my family's first *poor* Christmas when Dad was just getting out of the hospital and there was hardly anything under our tree except a few simple gifts from anonymous neighbors feeling sorry for us. I didn't get one thing that I could really brag about. Nothing! I remembered dreading going back to school at the end of Christmas vacation because I knew everyone was going to ask me, "What'd you get for Christmas?" How do you tell your friends that your family's so poor you didn't get one decent present? And the teachers always let everybody stand up in front of the class and brag about all their gifts. I actually prayed that I'd get sick and escape the embarrassment and humiliation.

"Christmas is okay," I muttered evasively, mustering an ostensible show of indifference. "I like getting out of school."

Jennilynn grinned, her eyes sparkling. "You'll love Christmas in Eagar."

I shuddered, fearful that this year's Christmas would be more dismal and plain than our last one in Logan had been, but I didn't want Jennilynn to know that. In fact, I was determined that no one in Eagar would ever know how totally poor we were.

ALMA J. YATES

CHAPTER 3

It was a disconcerting shock to discover that Jennilynn, my only friend in Eagar, was not the poor orphan that I had hoped she would be. Discouraged and despondent, I dragged home from her fancy place and dropped onto our front lawn. I didn't know how much money Dad was going to make working for Evan Slade, but I was positive that it wouldn't be enough. Our pitiful circumstances demanded extraordinary intervention, a tremendous amount of generosity from a very rich person. I suspected that the only person capable of that sort of generosity was Duchess Marge Thurman. My covetous imagination stirred and I realized that it would be an easy thing for Mrs. Thurman to demonstrate discreet pity and rescue our family from the humiliating depths of despair.

"Deenee," Dad called unexpectedly, using the pet name he'd given me years earlier. He came down the front steps. "I need to run our first month's rent over to Mrs. Thurman. Do you want to give me a little support?" he invited cheerily.

I bolted to my feet, thinking that this might be the perfect opportunity to get on Marge Thurman's good side. As we approached the huge oak door, I was impressed by its finely crafted detail. I wanted to lift the shiny golden knocker and let it clang loudly and formally onto the brass plate in the middle of the door, but Dad chose the more traditional and less-officious manner, merely pushing the doorbell. I heard the gentle, musical chime of the bell as it sounded throughout the house, and I strained to hear any approaching footsteps, but there was only silence. Dad dug his hands into his pockets and smiled down at me while I fidgeted nervously on the doorstep.

After a long silence, Dad rang the bell a second time. Once again the musical chimes echoed through the house's corridors, but it was only after the third ring that the giant door finally swung soundlessly inward—barely a foot. Out through the opening peered a narrow-faced, pale, imposing woman. Her coal black hair, obviously dyed, was wrapped about her head and fastened in a tight bun at the back. Greenish-gray, melancholy, unblinking eyes looked out from beneath her painted brows. Though her lips were brightly painted, her mouth was tight and unsmiling, and her nose long like one accustomed to the air of pomposity. I recognized her immediately as the woman at the cemetery.

ALMA J. YATES

Somewhat in awe, I stared, certain that I was seeing my first duchess in the flesh. In stature Mrs. Thurman was about five feet ten inches, somewhat slender in build, and a very distinguished figure. My attention was drawn to her long, delicate fingers grasping the door, the nails meticulously manicured and painted the same bright red as her lips.

"Hello," Dad greeted jocularly. "Mrs. Thurman, I assume."

For a prolonged moment, Marge Thurman stared imperiously. "May I help you?" she finally inquired in a deep, rigid, resonating voice.

"Ted Cluff here. My family and I moved into your place." He jerked a thumb over his shoulder. "This is my youngest daughter, Nadine." He put his arm across my shoulders. Mrs. Thurman didn't cast even a cursory glance in my direction. "I came to pay our first month's rent," Dad went on.

"I instructed Mr. Slade to have you mail the check to me each month," Mrs. Thurman said coolly, her eyes narrowing ever so slightly.

"Oh, it's no bother to bring the money to you," Dad offered, smiling.

"No bother . . . for whom?"

Dad chuckled. "Well, if you prefer, from now on I'll send the rent in the mail." He dug into his shirt pocket and extracted a check, folded over once.

Mrs. Thurman didn't even look at it. "I shall expect it prior to the first of every month. That was the arrangement I made with Mr. Slade." She started to close the door and then paused. "There is also the matter of the deposit and the last month's rent."

The smile wilted from Dad's face. "Evan thought we might work something out with you there. You see, we just moved from Utah. I don't start work till Monday. We're a little strapped for cash. The truth is, I don't have it right this moment."

"But, Mr. Cluff, you are living in my house. Right this moment. Correct?"

Dad's cheeks colored, and he glanced down at me. I could tell he was embarrassed. "Yes, that's true," he stammered, "and I certainly plan to get the money to you. Soon. I always pay my debts."

Mrs. Thurman nodded once. "I rented the little house against my better judgment, only after, shall we say, some pressure from your good friend Mr. Slade. Because he had performed several small favors for my late husband, he made me feel obligated." The door began to close again.

"Won't you take the check?" Dad asked, still holding it out.

Marge glanced down her nose at it, but only for a brief moment. "I believe I explained that I want the checks mailed to me." She took in a deep breath and raised her brows slightly. "Good afternoon, Mr. Cluff." The door began to close again, but Mrs. Thurman reconsidered and paused. "Do you have many children, Mr. Cluff?"

"Six," Dad answered proudly. "But only five are at home. I have a daughter in Denmark on a mission and—"

"Do you have many *young* children?" she interrupted, her eyes darting to me for a brief second. Before Dad could answer, she continued stiffly, "I take great pains to keep my yard up. During the summer months I hire a gardener. It is a rather large yard, and it may look almost like a small park. However, it is *not* a park for neighborhood children."

Dad pulled me close to him. "I'm sure we'll remember that."

Mrs. Thurman nodded ever so slightly, and the door began to close. But apparently she thought of one more thing. "Mr. Cluff," she said solemnly, "proximity makes us neighbors in a way, but I guard my privacy." She pressed her lips together as though pondering her next words. "I prefer that people not barge in unannounced."

Dad smiled humorlessly. "Mrs. Thurman, we'll definitely respect your privacy."

The corners of Mrs. Thurman's lips moved. It was difficult to determine whether the movement was upward or merely outward, but the movement or twitching was the only thing remotely resembling a smile that Mrs. Thurman had offered since opening her front door. "Thank you, Mr. Cluff." And with that she soundlessly closed the door.

For a moment both of us stared at the spot where Mrs. Thurman had once stood. Slowly, Dad tucked the check in his pocket and we started back home. "Deenee," he offered in a low voice, giving me a reassuring squeeze, "we can now say we've met our neighbor." He raised a forefinger. "I suspect it will be our first and last time."

"I think she's a real duchess," I remarked, still awed by our brief encounter with the mysterious, enigmatic Marge Thurman.

Dad smiled faintly. "Well, Deenee, I've never met a real duchess, but Mrs. Thurman does a marvelous impersonation."

* * *

Though Mrs. Thurman had seemed brusque and distant, and I left her door being a bit afraid of her, I was also convinced that if I could manage to get on her good side, she might warm up to me. Immediately I began concocting wonderful fantasies about her, thinking ahead to Christmas. Destitute of any other hopeful ideas, I began to imagine Mrs. Thurman being kind and generous, at least to me, and magically making my Christmas in Eagar a rich and exciting one.

Monday afternoon, after my first day at Round Valley Elementary School, I stole over to Mrs. Thurman's place, determined to catch her attention and worm my way into her heart. I had seen her white Cadillac disappear down the street in the direction of the cemetery, so, grabbing a rake from our garage, I charged across the street. Although Mrs. Thurman's yard had obviously been raked earlier in the fall, since then the last of the autumn leaves had fluttered to the ground around several of the trees. For the next hour I labored frantically, and soon the lawn was dotted with neat piles of crispy golden leaves.

Just as I was finishing under the last tree, one near the driveway, I spotted Mrs. Thurman's car. Wanting to appear busy, I raked vigorously. I heard the car pull into the driveway and stop a few feet from me. A moment later I heard the low hum of the automatic window rolling down.

"Young lady, what, may I ask, are you doing?"

"Oh, you're back," I gushed, straightening up and pretending to be surprised. "I thought I'd get done before you got back."

"Young lady, what *are* you doing?" The words held a sharp, suspicious edge.

"You still had leaves on your lawn, so I figured I'd clean them up for you."

"I distinctly remember explaining to your father that you were not to play here."

"Oh, but I'm working," I explained, taken aback by her cool, curt tone.

"You are trespassing." I could feel my smile droop under the onslaught of Mrs. Thurman's words. "Now what am I to do with all those . . . those unsightly piles cluttering my yard like . . . so many molehills?" Her exasperation was obvious.

"I'll pick up the piles," I offered frantically.

"And I suppose you'll want to be paid?"

I gulped. "I didn't do it for money," I practically pleaded, trying not to lie.

"There are two garbage containers in the garage. I'll set them out. Leave them by the back corner of the house. Carmelita can take them to the curb on trash pickup day."

Although I had expected a more favorable response from Mrs. Thurman, after the initial shock of her harsh words, I was still determined to win her over. I set about stuffing the leaves into trash barrels. While I labored, I glanced periodically toward the house, hoping to spot Mrs. Thurman watching me from one of the gabled second-floor windows, but I didn't see anyone.

When I finally lugged the last barrel to the corner of the house, the sun was dropping behind the western hills and there was a definite chill in the air. Unexpectedly, Mrs. Thurman emerged from her front door and stood imperiously with her hands clasped in front of her. "Young lady," she called to me, her tone all business.

ALMA J. YATES

I faced her hopefully, anticipating a gush of compliments, punctuated with words of apology for having doubted my ability and sincerity. "Yeah," I responded expectantly.

"I prefer not to repeat myself. I will make an exception today. My place is off limits. I do not want you playing here anymore."

"But I wasn't playing," I choked, pointing to the yard now free of leaves.

"Whatever you were doing, I didn't ask you to do it, and I don't want you doing it anymore. If I need assistance, I will hire someone capable of performing the task."

"But, Mrs. Thurman," I protested, "I was trying to help you."

"In the future, please don't try or I will have no alternative but to report you to the police. Do you understand?" I nodded, utterly astounded. Mrs. Thurman held out one of her hands. "This is all the change I have."

"But I didn't do it for money," I almost whimpered.

"Take the money and go." When I didn't move, she added sharply, "Quickly! I don't have all day. It's more than I should give you since I didn't request your services. Please don't assume that because I am paying you now that you may return."

Awkwardly I crept forward and held out my hand. Mrs. Thurman let several coins clink onto my open palm.

Without another word, she turned and disappeared soundlessly behind her ponderous oak door.

For a moment I stared through my tears at the closed door. My lower lip quivered, partly from the approaching evening chill, but mostly from Mrs. Thurman's harsh treatment. Hurt, humiliated, and devastated by the disintegration of my subtle plan to win Mrs. Thurman's heart and gain a bountiful Christmas, I swallowed and glanced down at the few coins in my hand—four pennies two nickels, a dime, and a single quarter.

Suddenly my tears dried up and my whole body swelled with eleven-year-old wrathful indignation. All my work for a grudging grand total of forty-nine cents! "You're no duchess," I spewed spitefully. "You're nothing but a rich, selfish old lady. I don't want your dirty money!" Rearing back, I hurled the coins into the empty flower bed next to the front steps.

CHAPTER 4

I was too embarrassed and humiliated to tell anyone in the family about my disastrous work detail for Mrs. Thurman, but I boiled inwardly and no longer harbored fantasies of receiving holiday help from our rich neighbor. I derived a certain sadistic delight, however, when Dad, Daniel, and Mom had similar experiences. The Friday before Thanksgiving, the phone rang during dinner. It was Mrs. Thurman asking for Dad. All at the table held our breath while Dad went to the phone. Actually, he didn't do a lot of talking. He mainly listened and nodded his head.

Returning to the table, he cast a puzzled glance out the kitchen window where we could see the lights from Mrs. Thurman's house glowing in the night. "She's expecting her son and family for Christmas. She wants Daniel and me to do some work tomorrow."

"Me?" Daniel protested. "Why'd she ask for me?"

Dad's mouth curled into an amused grin. "Actually, she didn't exactly ask for either one of us." He chuckled. "I'd say it was more like a summons. She did offer to pay." He sucked in a deep breath and exhaled slowly. "We could use the money."

Dad and Daniel spent all the next day trimming trees and shrubbery, digging up flower beds, sweeping off the back patio, and performing sundry other chores. They didn't drag home until almost dark.

"Did you earn lots of money?" Wendy inquired curiously.

Daniel pulled off his coat and tossed it on a kitchen chair. Dad cleared his throat and explained slowly, "She'll reduce our December rent."

"By a whopping fifteen big bucks," Daniel growled, his ears a flaming red.

The following Monday Mom received her summons. Carmelita Baca, Mrs. Thurman's hired help, was going to visit family in Mexico until the first of January, so Mrs. Thurman requested Mom's help during Carmelita's absence.

"Tell her no," Daniel suggested resentfully. "She won't pay you what you're worth."

"I've been thinking about Mrs. Thurman," Mom mused thoughtfully. "I've decided she needs a friend."

"The last thing she wants is a friend," I humphed. "Who would want to be her friend in the first place?"

"Maybe I do," Mom offered with a smile. "This will be my chance."

So Mom started working a couple of hours each day—cleaning Mrs. Thurman's home, doing laundry, and fixing at least one meal. In the beginning Mrs. Thurman hardly spoke to her, just enough to give succinct instructions on how everything was to be done. And much to Dad and Daniel's chagrin, Mrs. Thurman agreed to deduct twenty dollars from our rent for the hours Mom worked each week.

The Wednesday evening before Thanksgiving, Mom took dinner to Mrs. Thurman—hot rolls and beef stew. She enlisted my help to carry the food. It was the first time that I had returned to Mrs. Thurman's huge, forbidding front door since my work experience. When Mrs. Thurman answered the door and discovered us with dinner, she invited us in, but not past her spacious entryway. She had us set the food on a large credenza just inside the door, but I had a quick moment to look around.

The entryway floor was polished oak covered with a thick oriental rug. A high ceiling was adorned with a large crystal chandelier. There was a floor-to-ceiling mirror on each side of the wall, along with one large painting of an early American countryside. Straight ahead was a wide, carpeted staircase leading upstairs. Although I couldn't see the rest of the house, I had to assume that it was finely made and richly furnished.

"We'd love to have you for Thanksgiving dinner tomorrow," Mom invited.

I almost shouted a protest. Thanksgiving dinner was going to be bleak at best—chicken instead of turkey. I definitely didn't want to share our little bit with Marge Thurman. Fortunately, she rescued us from her own poor company by stiffly declining.

"Then we'll at least send a plate of food over," Mom offered congenially.

"If you wish," Mrs. Thurman conceded as though accepting Mom's meager offering was doing all of us a gigantic favor.

"She's not a very nice lady," I remarked on our way home.

"It isn't that she isn't nice. She's lonely but doesn't know how to reach out to others to cure her loneliness." Mom smiled. "She needs us, Nadine. She just doesn't know it yet."

I had no desire to get to know Marge Thurman, especially not during our Thanksgiving dinner. Fortunately Thanksgiving didn't turn out as bleak as I had dreaded. Mom roasted two small chickens, and we had piles of mashed potatoes and gravy, vegetables, dressing, cranberries, hot rolls, two kinds of salads, and pumpkin pies topped with fluffy whipped cream. Caught up in this simple abundance, I didn't dwell on our family's reduced financial circumstances. I even managed to be

ALMA J. YATES

relatively pleasant when Mom asked me to help carry plates of Thanksgiving dinner to Mrs. Thurman.

"I doubt she even wants this stuff," I complained as we trudged up the long driveway. "She probably doesn't eat regular food like the rest of us."

However, when Mrs. Thurman opened the door, she actually seemed pleased to see us. "I didn't think you would remember," she stated with the first traces of a smile that I had ever seen on her thin lips. It wasn't a bona fide smile like other people wear, but it was an improvement over the sour-faced scowl I'd grown accustomed to seeing.

"We missed having you for dinner," Mom said, setting her plate on the credenza. She wagged a finger at Mrs. Thurman. "I should have insisted. Next time I will."

"I don't believe I'll be here next Thanksgiving," was Marge's guarded reply.

"We won't wait till then," Mom countered. "We'll expect you for Christmas."

Mrs. Thurman's smile faded. "Speaking of Christmas," she said, clearing her throat somberly, "Willard liked to put up the Christmas lights right after Thanksgiving. I'd like to carry on his tradition. Besides, I'd like them up for my son and his family. Could you send Mr. Cluff over?"

Dad and Daniel weren't inclined to reenlist in Mrs. Thurman's cheap labor detail. In fact, they would have gladly declined had Mom not been firmly persuasive.

"Christmas is just around the corner," she pointed out, "and Christmas is about giving."

"It would be nice if Mrs. Thurman gave a little something," I volunteered sullenly. "She's got tons more to give than we do."

Mom countered gently but emphatically, "I don't believe Jesus said that we should give only when we have an abundance. The poorest peasant can still give something."

"I guess that's what we are," Daniel responded with a crooked grin. "We're probably the poorest bunch of peasants in all of Eagar."

"Well, my humble peasant," Mom joked, "the Lord will bless you for giving."

I wasn't convinced that blessings would rain down on us because Dad and Daniel did a simple service project for Marge Thurman. However, the day after they put up the Christmas lights and just as I was bracing myself for a holiday draped in gray shrouds of poverty, we received a sparkle of good news—Evan Slade presented Dad with a surprise Christmas bonus of $100, and the same day we unexpectedly received an insurance adjustment check in the mail for $75.

My hopes for a merry Christmas suddenly soared. Of course, I knew that even with our newly acquired "wealth" our Christmas would be modest compared to most people's. Jennilynn, for example, had already confided in me that she was practically positive that her parents were purchasing a color TV and a huge stereo system for her. My family's good fortune certainly couldn't compete with that kind of prosperity, but at least now I wouldn't wake up Christmas morning to a stocking bulging with food-storage rice, wheat, and dried lima beans.

The rest of the family was just as excited as I was. As a result, Dad announced that as part of our family's Monday home evening we would convene a family council to decide how to use the $175. Enthusiastically, I did some quick calculations, but my holiday euphoria soon soured into discouragement and self-pity. The miserable math left each family member a meager $21.87. Next to Jennilynn's TV and stereo, plus all her other predicted gifts, $21.87 bordered on destitution.

I considered other possibilities. Since Tammy was in Denmark, she didn't need to horn in on our Christmas money. Daniel would be buying bunches of stuff to get ready for his mission to Argentina. Of course, he would use his own hard-earned money, but still he'd have clothes galore, and they would be good for his Christmas gifts. I felt a twinge of guilt when I scratched Mom and Dad from the list, but I rationalized that they would probably want something boring like furniture, which was impossible with a mere $21.87 each. Eliminating those four family members produced a much more promising Christmas calculation—$43.74 each.

At first glance, $43.74 seemed a huge amount! But I couldn't help wondering how much Jennilynn's TV and stereo would cost. As I recalled what I'd seen in stores, the value of $43.74 diminished significantly. Then in the midst of this discouraging dilemma, I fantasized about the family giving me the whole amount! After all, they'd had more Christmases than I had.

* * *

Monday evening the season's first white sprinkles of snow fluttered from the gray sky, and a cold wind breathed against the black windowpane over the kitchen sink as Wendy and I hurried through the dinner dishes. I had devised a subtle plan. When Dad asked for my suggestion, I would pretend to ponder, then with a misty gaze, I'd say, "I just want to do whatever makes the family happiest. Even if just one person gets everything. That's fine with me. After all, Christmas is about making others happy."

I had even practiced enough so that with a little effort I could spice up my proposal with some teary emotion. After all, I wanted to go straight for their hearts, supposing that once the family witnessed my selfless proposal, they would all scramble to dedicate most, if not all, the Christmas money to me.

ALMA J. YATES

"Nadine, what do you want to do with the Christmas money?" Wendy questioned softly as she hefted a stack of plates to the cupboard.

I hesitated, debating whether to practice my emotional dramatics on Wendy before actually doing it for the whole family. Before I could decide, though, Wendy closed the cupboard and said, "There's this jumper and blouse in Karla's Fashion Shop."

"Clothes? For Christmas?" I asked, incredulous.

Wendy smiled dreamily. "Oh, there's a bunch of other things I'd want, but I don't think my part of the money will stretch that far." She clutched a damp dishtowel. "Do you ever dream of having . . ." She bit down on her lower lip and then burst out laughing. "Having all of it?" she exclaimed happily.

"You mean the whole $175?" I asked, alarmed.

My shock must have shown because Wendy quickly added, "I'm just being crazy, Deenee. I really think we should do something super nice for Tammy."

"Tammy!" I choked.

"Her first Christmas in Denmark she needs to know we're thinking of her."

"We'll write letters," I pointed out, not liking the direction of Wendy's plans. "I mean, she's into all that missionary stuff. She doesn't care about presents."

"And there's Daniel," Wendy went on. "This will be his last Christmas here."

"But he'll get gobs of stuff for his mission. We shouldn't waste—I mean, spend—that little bit of money on him. He can't use Christmas presents now."

Before we could discuss the money further, Mom called us into the living room for family home evening. Immediately I sensed something amiss. Dad and Daniel had both been rather somber and reticent during dinner, but I just assumed they'd had a tough workday. Now Mom was solemn and subdued as well, which wasn't like her. Worriedly I squeezed onto the sofa between Wendy and Daniel.

"Before home evening," Dad announced, "I have a bit of bad news." He cleared his throat and glanced across the room at Mom, who stared at her hands folded in her lap. "We'd planned to discuss how to spend our extra money for Christmas." He shook his head ruefully. "It doesn't look like we'll have that discussion tonight."

An ugly worm of misgiving wriggled inside me. "But why?" I wanted to know.

"We decided to give poor Mrs. Thurman a little Christmas bonus," Daniel grumbled sarcastically. "We don't want her to go without."

"Mrs. Thurman!" I exploded. "She's the last person on earth to get our money."

"Actually, she's going to be the first," Daniel muttered dryly.

I glanced between Dad and Daniel. Finally Dad nodded slowly. "Daniel and I stopped by Mrs. Thurman's place just before supper to fix a few of the strands of Christmas lights." He fidgeted in his chair. "She reminded us that we still haven't paid our deposit or our last month's rent. She would like it by the end of the week."

"And how much is that?" Rusty asked glumly.

Dad heaved a tired sigh. "One hundred and eighty dollars."

"She doesn't have a right to ask for that money now," Wendy spoke up. "I mean, it's Christmas! What are we supposed to do? What's she thinking?"

"Well, she's sure not thinking about *your* Christmas," Daniel muttered.

"We should have paid everything before we ever moved in," Mom explained gently, speaking for the first time. "Mrs. Thurman did us a giant favor when she let us move in without paying the deposit and last month's rent."

"One hundred and eighty dollars," I protested loudly. "That's *all* our Christmas money. Why does she need the money right now?"

"Poodles," Daniel said simply.

"Poodles?" the rest of us asked in surprised unison.

"Her excuse for asking for the money now is that she wants to buy two poodles for her granddaughters without taking money out of the bank."

"One hundred and eighty dollars for a couple of dumb dogs?" Garrett shrieked.

"Each one is registered and pretty uppity when it comes to dogs," Daniel explained. "She claims she's getting a real bargain at seventy-five dollars per dog. One's white and one's black. A matched pair. Then she wants to buy them collars, leashes, coats, and a few other little things. I figured you'd all be excited to help Mrs. Thurman buy her poodles. Where's your Christmas spirit, anyway?" he asked with sarcasm.

"He's kidding, isn't he, Dad?" Wendy questioned.

Dad shook his head. "I'm afraid not. Mrs. Thurman has a son who lives in Boston," he explained. "He's an executive in a brokerage firm. He has twin girls about ten years old who have always gotten whatever they want. Mrs. Thurman wants to get something unique, something they don't already have. She thought poodles would do the trick."

"Poodles?" I gasped, practically gagging.

"We were going to have Christmas a long time before we ever knew about the extra money," Mom pointed out with her usual unflappable aplomb, smiling for the first time. I knew she was just trying to make the rest of us feel better. She failed miserably.

"Christmas has never been about money," Mom went on. "It's about giving. Unfortunately, too many people have made money into a Christmas crutch. They believe—

very wrongly, I might add—that unless they have money, they can't have Christmas." She shook her head. "The first Christmas didn't have anything to do with money. Jesus didn't have any money in that cold manger."

"But he got gold, frankincense, and myrrh," Garrett pointed out. "We don't get anything."

Mom smiled. "But isn't it interesting that we don't know what happened to those first gifts? The giving that Christ did later didn't have anything to do with gold or money. The true spirit of Christmas is never about giving money, kids. Perhaps without the money we will be able to discover for ourselves true Christmas giving."

"Oh, please, Mom," Wendy muttered, rolling her eyes.

"This is all crazy," I sputtered, fighting back tears as a wave of anger washed over me. I wanted to press my hands to my ears and block out everything Mom was saying. Nothing she could say would change the fact that our family's good fortune had been harshly swallowed up by Mrs. Thurman's voracious selfishness.

"When we decided to hold this family council, it was to plan Christmas," Mom reminded us with annoying optimism. "We can still do that." She smiled broadly. "Let's make plans with what we have. This could all be a blessing in disguise."

"This is one blessing that's definitely disguised," Wendy murmured.

"How about making gifts for each other?" Mom went on, refusing to allow the family's discouragement to dampen her spirits. "Those gifts come from our hearts."

"And go straight to the dump the day after Christmas," Garrett said under his breath.

"Garrett," Mom cautioned before pressing on. "My most memorable gifts are the ones you've all made for me. When Rusty was a Cub Scout, he gave me a set of plaster bookends taken from a mold of his very own hands. I love them."

"Great!" I burst out. "I'll tell everybody at school that I got a pair of Rusty's plaster hands for Christmas. I'm sure they'll all be so impressed."

"Actually," Rusty snickered, "every girl in your school probably wants a pair of these hands." He held his hands out in front of him and pretended to admire them. He nudged Wendy with his toe. "Wendy, how many pairs of my hands do you want?"

Wendy kicked at Rusty's foot and snapped, "Stop being annoying!"

"I remember in *The Little House on the Prairie* books," Garrett volunteered, his face serious and thoughtful. "One Christmas the family got snowed in and didn't think they were getting anything for Christmas. Then this guy showed up and brought each of the kids something like an orange and a tin cup. They were really thankful." He struggled mightily to keep a revealing smirk from his face. I wanted to punch him for trying to be funny at a time like this.

"I think I can get everybody a cup." Rusty smiled. "I'll make them out of tin cans and decorate them with newspaper." He heaved a sigh. "Don't count on the orange, though, because oranges cost money. Deenee, do you want your cup made out of a Del Monte corn can or a Green Giant spinach can?"

"I'm not staying here and listening to Rusty's and Garrett's stupid jokes," I cried, pushing to my feet and charging from the room. I didn't want to cry, but once I reached my room I couldn't help it. I went to the window, pulled back the curtains, and glared toward Marge Thurman's house, which was ablaze with hundreds of colored Christmas lights, lights that Dad and Daniel had put up for her. "Poodles!" I snarled through clenched teeth. "Marge Thurman, I hope you have the most miserable Christmas of your life, and I hope your granddaughters hate poodles!"

CHAPTER 5

"You asleep, Deenee?" Wendy asked, slipping into the bedroom and flipping on the light.

Stewing morosely in my misery, I mumbled, "No, I'm awake."

Wendy's box springs creaked and squeaked as she crashed onto her bed. "Bummer," she grumbled. "I wonder if Marge Thurman knows how horribly selfish she is." She heaved a petulant sigh. "I'd like to give her a great big piece of my mind."

"Nothing would change," I lamented mournfully.

There was a soft knock at the door and then Mom pushed it open and stepped in. She came over to my bed and sat down, gently patting my shoulder through the covers. "I'm sorry," she remarked. Smiling ruefully, she added, "Ever since finding out about our extra money, I've been making a long list of gifts I wanted to buy for all of you. Of course, there wasn't enough money for everything I wanted," she admitted with an embarrassed smile, "but it was a good start." She laughed. "Dreaming was almost as fun as actually going out and buying things."

"I don't know why we had to end up with such a selfish neighbor," I responded, hoping my voice wouldn't crack. I didn't want to cry in front of Mom and Wendy.

"I don't know all the reasons Mrs. Thurman is the way she is," Mom explained after a long pause. "But she opened up to me today. It was as though she were dying to talk to someone, and once she started . . ." Mom took in a deep breath. "I think I understand her a little better now. I'm going to tell you about her so you'll understand her better too. Marge grew up in a very well-to-do family, but she was terribly shy and afraid of people. I think she was a bit of a recluse even as a young girl. To make matters worse, she had a younger sister who was beautiful, charming, and outgoing."

Poor Marge, I thought spitefully.

Mom smiled at my scowl and kept going. "She admitted that her family was shocked when she'd married Willard. He was poor and not the handsome, dashing type, but according to Marge he was a wonderful man and treated her royally. Her parents were so opposed to the marriage that they basically disowned her, at least for several years. During those years, Willard worked hard and was ingenious with investments. Before long he was practically as prosperous as his in-laws.

"Marge depended very much on Willard. She was still very awkward and nervous in public, so when he died last year, it was like her whole world crumbled around her."

"Does that give her the right to steal our Christmas money?" I questioned sullenly.

Mom sighed. "Nadine, she's not stealing, and like I said tonight, Christmas shouldn't be about money."

"It sure doesn't hurt to have some," I argued bitterly.

"Well, girls, I suppose we can mope around and moan and groan, or we can make other plans. How do we make this Christmas extra special?"

I glared at the floor, the wall, the ceiling, everywhere but at Mom. It was bad enough that our holiday had been pilfered; the last thing I wanted was for Mom to send me on a guilt trip or force me to embrace some ridiculously simple ray of concocted hope.

"People talk about the spirit of Christmas," Mom went on, "but not very many of us really discover it." I rolled my eyes, but Mom was undaunted. "Christmas isn't about how much we get. It's about—"

"How much we give," I broke in mockingly, punching my pillow with an ugly scowl on my face. "Please, Mom, just leave it alone."

Mom shrugged. "I'm convinced that our very best Christmases are the ones where we discover the Savior's secret of giving. He didn't ever give things—not things that were bought in a store with money, anyway—but He still gave. He gave so much to all of us. That's what Christmas is about, giving the way He gave. That's what I'm going to try to do—see how much I can truly give this Christmas." She pushed up from the bed. "I'm determined that this is going to be a wonderful Christmas."

"Do you want a pair of my plaster hands?" I muttered, holding up my hands. I let them drop onto the bed and added, "Let's all give hands this Christmas. The whole house can be full of gold plaster hands. This will be our golden-hands Christmas."

Mom smiled, stood up, and started for the door. "If you want to give me a pair of golden hands," she remarked over her shoulder as she slipped out into the hall, "I'll treasure them."

The next day as Jennilynn and I walked to school, I was past mourning and well into a silent state of depression. Jennilynn bubbled irritatingly with cheery holiday anticipation. "I really think this will be my best Christmas," she gushed, grinning. "I thought the TV and stereo were my big gifts." She closed her eyes dreamily and took in a deep breath of cold morning air.

"They're not?" My mouth dropped open.

Jennilynn looked around as though afraid someone might overhear her. "I think Mom and Dad have something else planned. Something really big!"

"Something *really* big?" I almost choked. "Something more than the TV and stereo? What are they going to do, get you your own car?"

"I'm not positive sure, but I think we're going to Disneyland and Sea World. I heard them talking last night. Dad doesn't know how to whisper so I heard everything. We went to Disneyland a few years ago, but all I remember is throwing up in the parking lot."

"I hope you have a better time this Christmas," I responded without enthusiasm. "Our family will be doing tons of fun things too," I remarked, not wanting Jennilynn to suspect how dismal our celebration was going to be. I was glad Jennilynn would be in Disneyland so she wouldn't discover my family's horrible holiday secret.

Then, without warning, Jennilynn punched me with a staggering question. "What are *you* getting this Christmas? You've got to have some idea. Tell me!"

I knew full well there was no possible way that I could confess my family's poverty to Jennilynn. The only thing worse than actually being poor was having your friends know about it. I gulped and groped helplessly for an evasive response, but all I managed to latch onto without advance notice—excluding, of course, a blatant black lie—was Mom's insipid suggestion from the night before. "Well, as a family we've been thinking about . . . well, you know, we'll be . . ." I looked away, scrambling to think of a plausible way to make Mom's ridiculous plan sound inviting to someone who was going to receive a TV, a stereo, and a trip to Disneyland.

"Before we moved here, we had some really cool Christmases with tons of stuff," I ventured exuberantly, hoping that I wasn't lying as much as being colorfully creative. I wct my lips. "But what my family really likes to do at Christmastime is . . ." I coughed. "Well, we're going to . . ." I shook my head. "We're not getting each other expensive gifts. We've tried that tons of times. This year we're trying to . . ." I chewed on my lower lip and felt my cheeks burn guiltily. "We're going to get into the . . ." I struggled to find the right words. "Well, we're doing the giving thing this Christmas," I burst out in exasperation. I choked, finding it hard to swallow. "Actually, we do it all the time, you know, the giving thing, I mean. It really makes Christmas more . . ." Suddenly I felt dizzy. "Well, more wonderful." I shook my head. Was I really saying these things or was this just like one of those obnoxious dreams where you discover that you're running around town with nothing on except your most ragged pair of underwear?

"The giving thing?" Jennilynn asked slowly, looking over at me, confusion as well as interest showing on her face. "What do you mean by the giving thing?"

I felt I was breaking out into a full-fledged fever. "Well, it's pretty simple," I stammered. "Nothing to it.

We give things to each other. We try to make each other happy. That's the whole point of the giving thing." I gulped and wet my lips. "You know, to give."

Jennilynn cocked her head to one side and scrunched up her nose in obvious perplexity. "I thought that's what everybody did at Christmas. I guess we've always done your *giving thing*. This year I'm giving Dad an electric shaver, and I'm giving Mom—"

"Not *that* kind of giving," I burst out, sorry now that I had dragged Mom's ridiculously crazy suggestion into this conversation with Jennilynn. Mom's suggestion had sounded lame the night before, but now it sounded totally stupid. I forced myself to smile, but I knew that there was absolutely no way that I was going to make Mom's Christmas concoction sound even remotely feasible, much less appealing. "That's the kind of giving everybody does—the store-bought kind of giving. That's what everybody does." I was repeating myself and could feel my cheeks burn hot red. "You see, we're not going to *buy* things. We're going to *make* them." I searched desperately for some way to make this absurd *giving thing* sound complex as well as intriguing. I ran my tongue over my lips to buy more time so that I could further fabricate this fantastic charade. And yet, all the while I instinctively suspected Jennilynn wasn't going to buy this.

"If you actually make something with your own hands—I mean, you think up the idea in your own head and figure out how to make it—then when you give that extra-special gift, you're really giving something of yourself, and that makes the whole idea of Christmas giving much more meaningful. It doesn't take anything to get something from the store. The giving thing is real, true giving," I concluded on a sugary note.

I didn't dare look at Jennilynn. I knew that one glance into her doubting eyes and I'd be forced to admit that I'd been caught in a huge holiday lie. "I know I'm not very good at explaining this," I spluttered, feeling guilty as well as exhausted. I gulped to catch my breath. "But the giving thing is really great! That's the whole reason why I'm not buying anything for anyone. I'm making my Christmas gifts."

"Making them?" Jennilynn's tone didn't hide her suspicious doubts. "Making what?"

"Oh, things that come from the heart," I answered. For a fleeting moment I coveted Mom's unabashed optimism. "Things that show you care about the other person." I felt like such a hypocrite because I didn't believe a single word I was saying. In fact, I had no desire to believe.

"Dad's always wanted this electric shaver," Jennilynn replied thoughtfully. "Mom helped me pick it out. And Mom wants this—"

"But, Jennilynn, you can't buy things and do the giving thing," I pressed forward. "You've got to make the gifts yourself because then you're giving a little bit of yourself. That's what makes the gift so special. When your dad gets that old shaver, he'll use it all right, but when it breaks, he'll just throw it away because it won't mean anything anymore. But if you give him something that you make, it won't matter how beat-up and broken it gets. He'll always keep it because it's a piece of you. I mean, this whole thing sounds plenty crazy, but it really works. It's not for everybody, though," I quickly added. "Of course, you'll still want your TV and stuff, but you can really do some fun giving things," I lied desperately, filling my voice with fake, far-fetched enthusiasm that felt like thick, rancid syrup in my mouth.

Jennilynn managed to be polite. She looked away and shrugged. Then, unexpectedly, she asked, "What are you making for Rusty?"

I should have known Jennilynn would ask about my brother Rusty because she had a crazy crush on him. I pulled my coat tighter around myself to stall for time. "I'll make him a really nice . . ." I chewed on my lower lip. In my entire life, I had never considered making anything for one of my brothers. "A really nice gym bag," I burst out. I don't know why I said *gym bag*. Why didn't I say a really nice beanie, a cool book marker, or a nifty glove bag, something I might have thrown together in fifteen minutes? Shoot, I didn't even know how to make a gym bag, but Rusty had mentioned to Mom that he needed a gym bag.

"He wants a gym bag for Christmas?" Jennilynn raised her eyebrows.

I wanted to crawl into a deep, dark hole, but I didn't retreat. Pride wouldn't let me, so I blundered forward. "Oh, it won't be an ordinary bag," I explained, ashamed to even look at Jennilynn. "It'll have special compartments and pockets and his name on the side and . . ."

"What are you doing for Garrett?"

I sucked in a quick breath of icy morning air. "Well, I'm making Garrett a gym bag too. Rusty and Garrett are both into sports and stuff." I shrugged. "I mean, Jen, this is going to be a super bag, not like the cheap things you grab at Kmart."

Jennilynn stared straight ahead. "Will Wendy want a gym bag too?"

I thought later that I should have burst out laughing and told the truth, admitted that this whole thing was a farce, but I didn't. "Don't be a goof, Jen," I laughed nervously. "I have this really neat idea for a dry arrangement." I knew if I said "neat" or "super" one more time to describe these imaginary gifts, I'd yank out my own tongue by the roots.

Jennilynn paused. "A dry arrangement? Do you even know how to make one?"

I remembered a simple arrangement I'd thrown together in second grade for Mother's Day—a few dried weeds and some sticks and rocks held together by gobs

ALMA J. YATES

of cheap molding clay. Before the end of the week I had secretly tossed the ugly thing into the garbage because it was falling apart, and I was afraid Mom would keep it around indefinitely just because I'd made it. "I've made some really neat dry arrangements."

"I like the one on your coffee table," Jennilynn remarked. "Did you make that one?"

"Mom bought that one at Kmart," I grumbled. "The one I make for Wendy will be way better than that dumb one on the coffee table."

"Are you doing anything for Daniel? He probably won't need a gym bag on his mission."

I wanted to punch Jennilynn. I wondered why she kept this thing going. Was she just trying to torment me, or was she forcing me to admit that my family was shamefully and hopelessly impoverished? But I refused to retract anything.

"Daniel's going to be away from home for two years. He'll want a real cool framed picture of the family, one of those kinds with the padded fabric around it."

Taking a deep breath, I spoke again before Jennilynn could interrogate me further. "And Mom and Dad's gift will be the best and neatest of all. I'm making them a really super quilt."

"You mean a blanket?"

"Not a blanket! A quilt."

"Have you ever made a quilt?" Jennilynn asked slowly.

"No," I stammered, finally being honest after a long string of fabricated exaggerations. "But Sister Mercer, our Primary teacher, makes quilts. I'm sure she'll help me." I took another breath and added before Jennilynn could ask any more questions, "And since Tammy's in Denmark, I'll write her one long letter every month. She loves letters more than anything."

I looked away bitterly and was tempted to add, "Are you satisfied now? Do I have to answer any more of your dumb, stupid, idiotic questions?" I walked angrily but stoically. I almost longed to be back in Logan where my friends at least suspected that my family had fallen on hard times. I resolved never to discuss Christmas with Jennilynn again.

"You know, Nadine," Jennilynn finally said softly, "I wish I was like you and had a family like yours." She quickly shook her head. "Don't get me wrong. I mean, my family's okay, but there's just me and Mom and Dad. I get lots of things for Christmas, but they're just store-bought things. You're right about those things not meaning much." She thought a moment, her head cocked to one side. "You know, I can't even remember what I got for Christmas last year. I got a bike, but I'm not sure if it was last year or the year before. I wish my family did something like the giving thing." She shook her head. "But Mom and Dad are so busy that they don't have time for something like the giving thing."

I stiffened, not sure if Jennilynn was mocking me. I looked over at her. She looked back at me through a thin mist of seemingly genuine tears, then reached out and touched my arm. "I don't think my family will ever do nice things for Christmas like yours does. We'll just keep right on buying stuff that doesn't mean anything. In a couple of months, Dad won't even remember I bought that electric shaver. But every time your mom and dad see that quilt, they'll think of you. Yours is the kind of Christmas I'd like."

My mouth dropped open. I wanted to burst out, "You can have it! All of it. I'll trade you straight across. I already know where I'd put your TV and stereo." But I also felt dumbfounded as I studied Jennilynn. I realized that unless she was the world's greatest pretender, she wasn't mocking me. She was envious. Jennilynn Lewis, who had everything, wanted my cheap Christmas.

"Oh, Jen, don't be a dope. Your Christmas is just fine. Besides," I stammered in shocked amazement, "Mom's the one that thought up this whole giving thing."

"You have a cool mom," Jennilynn said softly. We walked in silence, and I watched my steamy breath puff out in front of my face, feeling terribly guilty the whole while for taking advantage of Jennilynn's innocent gullibility. Besides, I knew I wasn't going to make gym bags, picture frames, dry arrangements, or a quilt. "Could

I ask a huge favor?" Jennilyn added, still in a quiet voice. Before I could respond, she pushed on. "I promise to do whatever you say."

"What are you talking about?" I questioned, totally baffled.

"Can I help you make the gifts?" She stopped and grabbed me by the arm. "I've never done the giving thing before."

"Huh?" I wouldn't have been more shocked had Jennilynn kicked off her shoes and socks and danced down the icy pavement in her bare feet.

"Can't you use a little help?" She was genuinely excited. "I'll bet that Mom's got some material at the variety store for the gym bags and the quilt."

"Jennilynn Lewis, you're so weird," I muttered.

"Please, Nadine. Maybe I can learn to do the giving thing too."

I looked away, my mouth sagging open, the cold morning air freezing my teeth. Slowly I shrugged. "Yeah, I guess that'd be all right." As soon as I gave my limp permission, I wanted to shake my head and shout, "What am I saying? This is stupid! I'm not doing any of these things." But I couldn't confess to Jennilynn that I had told such a big, whopping lie.

All during school I thought about the incredulous Christmas that I had spontaneously masterminded. I hoped that by noon Jennilynn would turn her thoughts to her TV, stereo, and trip to Disneyland and forget everything that had been said about the giving thing.

Unfortunately, at lunchtime the giving thing was all Jennilynn wanted to talk about. She pulled me to one of the wooden benches on the far side of the playground and insisted that we make Christmas plans.

That evening I was more depressed than ever as I wondered how I could rationally break the news to Jennilynn that the giving thing was just a ridiculous brainchild born of desperation and shame.

CHAPTER 6

Although Mom first went to Mrs. Thurman's house as a common laborer, something tantamount to a servant, it wasn't long before Mrs. Thurman warmed up to her, and the two of them became friends in a strange kind of way. Even on days when she didn't have to work, Mom regularly visited the rich old lady. Occasionally Mom would bake rolls, bread, or other treats to share with Mrs. Thurman. Too often for my liking, I got stuck with the distasteful task of delivering the goods. Mrs. Thurman was never friendly with me. I suspected she was disappointed that Mom wasn't the one to appear at her door.

For a short time after Dad surrendered our Christmas money to Mrs. Thurman and Mom became her friend, I secretly hoped that Mrs. Thurman's heart would soften and she would rescue us from our pending pauper's Christmas. Unfortunately, it didn't seem to matter how many nice things Mom did for Mrs. Thurman, she never gave any indication that she might reciprocate in any way other than a meager deduction in our monthly rent. Eventually I accepted the fact that we were destined to have a horrible holiday. The night I arrived at that bleak conclusion, I went to bed more dejected than I'd been since arriving in Eagar. I buried my face in my pillow and cried.

"What's wrong, Deenee?" Wendy asked as she slipped into the bedroom later that night and heard my muffled sniffles.

"Nothing," I managed, choking back my grief. "Everything's fine, just wonderful," I answered, fighting bravely to hold my voice steady but facing the wall so Wendy couldn't see my red, puffy eyes. I hadn't planned to say more, but my bitter disappointment was too great and I snapped sarcastically, "I'm just so excited about the cool Christmas we're going to have." Then the tear ducts burst, and I bawled in earnest.

For a moment Wendy didn't say anything. Then she stepped over to my bed, dropped down next to me, and stroked my shoulder. "Don't cry, Nadine." I was surprised by how gentle she sounded. "I wish I had something to . . ." She bent over and hugged me. "I wish we still had the money. I'd vote to give it all to you." She sounded totally sincere.

"It isn't fair," I whimpered. "Why does all the bad stuff have to happen to us? I thought things would get better here in Arizona, but they're getting worse."

"I'm sorry, Nadine," Wendy answered softly. "I really am."

I think that night was the first time I realized that Wendy sincerely cared about me. With my heart melting, I turned and put my arms around her neck and squeezed as tears ran down my cheeks. Suddenly I thought of the dry arrangement that I had told Jennilynn I was going to make for Wendy, the one I had never seriously considered making. That simple dry arrangement seemed so insignificant now, but as Wendy held me and I hugged her back, I was determined to somehow show Wendy that I cared about her too. I'd make that dry arrangement—and make it even better than I had described it for Jennilynn.

The following Sunday was a gray, bleak day. I wasn't even thinking of Christmas when, after church, Wendy brought Jennilynn to my bedroom and showed her in. I was lying on the bed staring blankly at a book while I felt sorry for myself. "Shall we start everything today?" Jennilynn asked in a whisper, smiling broadly as she closed the door behind her so Wendy couldn't hear.

"Start what today?" I stammered, not knowing what she was talking about and shocked that she was actually standing in my bedroom on a Sunday afternoon.

"You said I could help," she bubbled secretively, creeping over to my bed. "At least you didn't say I couldn't." Seeing my shock, she explained quietly, "I'm here to make Christmas gifts." For a moment a shadow of dread darkened her face. "You haven't finished, have you?"

My mouth sagged open. "I didn't say I was doing anything today," I started.

"But Christmas is only three weeks away," she pointed out. "What do we do first?"

"I . . . well, I guess we . . . but, Jen, I haven't had time to think much about anything," I burst out in exasperation, feeling a bit lightheaded as I gasped for breath.

"No time to think?" Jennilynn came back. "You've had tons of time." She shook her head and grinned. "Your giving thing is all I've thought about. How about Rusty's gym bag?"

"Jen," I muttered, pushing off the bed and pacing the floor, "when I talked to you the other day, I was . . ." I hesitated, tempted to tell Jennilynn the whole horrible truth so this farce wouldn't go any further, but when I saw the hungry look of anticipation on her beaming face, I didn't have the heart to dash her hopes. I raked my fingers through my hair. "Jen, those gifts I told you about were . . ."

"You just want to make them yourself," Jennilynn whispered disappointedly. "And if I help, I'm butting in on your giving thing. I hadn't thought of that."

"No, it's not that exactly." I stared sadly at the floor.

"I'd probably feel the same way." She heaved a plaintive sigh. "I was just hoping that maybe this once I could help because I've never done the giving thing. I thought that maybe you could kind of show me the first time so . . ." Her words drifted off into silent disappointment.

"Jen, I'd love to have you help me," I burst out. "In fact, it would make it a lot easier." I winced. "But you see I'm still trying to figure out this giving thing myself."

Jennilynn's face brightened. "So it wouldn't ruin things if I helped?"

I felt a sinking in my stomach, knowing I was being dragged relentlessly into this pickle, but I didn't know how to extricate myself. At least, not yet. "Actually," I began, making a blind stab at honesty, "I don't have stuff for Rusty's gym bag, but I've thought a lot about Wendy's dry arrangement. I really do want to make a super nice arrangement for her, and we could start that today."

Jennilynn pressed her lips together and then burst out. "I hope you don't mind, but I asked Mom about some stuff you could use for a gym bag." She shook her head in anticipation of my protest. "I didn't say anything about the giving thing, but Mom said denim would work best." Jennilynn licked her lips and pressed on. "She's got some down at the variety store and said I could have what I wanted. We can get it after school tomorrow."

For a long time I studied Jennilynn, feeling a gentle tug at my heart. I actually felt like reaching out and hugging her. Instead I said quietly, "That'd be great, Jen."

Jennilynn grinned broadly. "So what do we need for Wendy's dry arrangement?"

I smiled. "Just dried things—weeds, grass, flowers, sticks, rocks—anything that will make an arrangement. We get the stuff first, then we make it into something."

Jennilynn's enthusiasm was so contagious that I began to wonder if perhaps there really was something magical about this giving thing I'd desperately devised. Bundled up in coats, sweaters, caps, and gloves, and carrying brown paper sacks, we marched to the edge of town to a huge field along the foothills where dried weeds, grass, sticks, and multishaped, colored rocks were in abundance. Soon we were in a contest to see who could find the most unusual and creative things for Wendy's dry arrangement.

With our arms and sacks loaded with the very best formed and preserved items, Jennilynn remembered a terrific basket that her mother had purchased months earlier at a yard sale but which now sat unused in their basement. She generously donated it to our Christmas cause, pending her mother's approval, and when we stopped by Jennilynn's home to pick up the basket, Mrs. Lewis offered a half dozen dried, long-stem roses that she had preserved from an old bouquet. She even let us spread everything out on a table in their basement family room, and then the three of us worked feverishly on Wendy's dry arrangement.

The next day Jennilynn and I stopped by the Lewises' variety store, where Mrs. Lewis gave us several large remnants of black denim. She even found a pattern for a tote bag, one that had been sitting on a back shelf. She quickly made some adjustments to the pattern and said, "If you two cut out the pieces, I'll help you sew everything together. I've got a sewing machine that works well on heavy fabric."

Standing in the Lewises' variety store and studying the neat bolts of cloth on the shelves, I felt my enthusiasm for the giving thing grow. Mrs. Lewis had already been more than generous and helpful, but I ventured one more request. "Do you have material for a quilt?" I asked, afraid I was being too bold. Mrs. Lewis looked at me askance, so I quickly added, "I'll pay for it. I don't have the money right now, but I'll earn it somehow."

"She's making a Christmas quilt for her parents," Jennilynn explained. She pressed her lips together and scrunched up her nose, deep in thought. "You've been saying that the back storeroom needs to be cleaned and organized. We'll do it! Please!"

Mrs. Lewis smiled. "You fix up the back room and you can choose your material."

I found it strange that once Jennilynn and I had embarked on our crazy Christmas crusade, my ridiculous giving thing seemed to take shape in a way that I'd never imagined. The following Saturday we went to work straightening and cleaning the variety store's back room. It was a bigger project than either of us had anticipated, but we were determined and finally finished. Mrs. Lewis took me to the fabric section and let me pick out my favorite material. I wanted something soft and warm, so I selected a soft flannel, something that I knew Mom and Dad would love curling up in. Mrs. Lewis also let me take a spongy roll of fluffy, white batting.

Even though I had the materials to make it, the quilt would have probably never happened without Jennilynn's help. The day after cleaning the variety store, I was having serious doubts about being able to actually make a quilt when Jennilynn called. "Everything's set. We start on the quilt tomorrow," she whispered earnestly.

"Look, Jen," I protested, fidgeting uneasily, "I just don't know if I can actually make a quilt. I've been doing some serious thinking," I stammered. "I should probably just make something that I can do by myself, something easy like . . ." I knit my brow and struggled to think of another plausible gift. "Something like plaster hands. I can paint them gold," I muttered, unable to think of

ALMA J. YATES

anything else. "I hate to break this to you, Jen, but I don't have a clue about making quilts."

"Plaster hands!" Jennilynn choked on the other end of the line. "Definitely not! You're making a quilt, and we're starting tomorrow. I've got everything planned."

"What?" I grumbled, glaring at the phone. I pressed the phone back to my ear. "How do we start tomorrow?" I muttered honestly. "Making a quilt isn't like throwing a bunch of dried weeds and grass together."

"I talked to Sister Mercer after church today. I couldn't believe you hadn't said anything to her about it yet. When I told her about your Christmas quilt, she got so excited. She's made tons of quilts. She'll have her quilting frames set up in her basement. We'll go there right after school, and she'll show us what to do." Jennilynn heaved a sigh. "I just love this giving thing."

It was strange, but Jennilynn's enthusiastic persistence won me over with this as well, and the following day Jennilynn and I showed up at Sister Mercer's place. The first time I sat down to work on the quilt after it had been mounted on the wooden frames, I grabbed the needle and wielded it like it was an ice pick. "Nadine," Sister Mercer cautioned, smiling and touching my shoulder, "quilting is delicate, dainty work. It takes finesse."

Jennilynn snickered, and I glared at her while Sister Mercer demonstrated a slow, deliberate sewing motion. "But that'll take forever," I grumbled, exasperated.

"But it'll be something your folks want on their bed instead of on their garage floor."

I had a lazy streak when it came to sewing. I just wanted to get finished, but Sister Mercer was emphatically persistent, refusing to tolerate carelessness. Surprisingly, Jennilynn caught on fast, but it took Sister Mercer's patient prodding to get me to the same point.

Our quilting project was given a huge boost when Wendy showed up late one afternoon. I had secretly told her about the quilt, and she was curious to see it. She had planned to drop by for just a moment, but she took up a needle and went to work along with the rest of us.

* * *

One evening a week or so before Christmas, when Jennilynn and I were laboring late on the quilt, she paused and surveyed our work. The quilt was huge, made of flannel, a holiday plaid of red, white, and green. It was stuffed with a generous amount of batting because I wanted this quilt to be warm, soft, and fluffy. "I wish I had something like this for Mom and Dad," Jennilynn mused. Longingly she touched the soft quilt stretched out on the wooden frames. "Dad will like his shaver and Mom her makeup kit, but . . ." Turning to me, she gushed with a sudden mist in her eyes, "I always thought I knew how to give good Christmas presents, but I didn't have a clue. Not until you showed me the giving thing."

"Oh, hush up, you dope. You always say the dumbest things."

"But it's true, Nadine."

I ducked my head, feeling my neck and ears burn guiltily. "Mom and Dad will like this quilt all right," I muttered, "but it's still just an old blanket."

"They'll love it, Nadine. I wish I was like you."

"Like me?" I asked, puzzled.

"You're so unselfish."

I almost choked, knowing the awful truth. "Actually, Jen," I started honestly, "I'm not all that unselfish. In fact, I think it would be safe to say—"

"But you *are*, Nadine. I love your giving thing. I want to do it every Christmas."

I squirmed uneasily. Oh, making Christmas gifts for my family had softened me, and I'd even learned to enjoy making them, but I knew that any genuine charity I'd mustered had been squeezed out of me by Jennilynn— drop by slow drop. With all her romantic exuberance, she had been the one to make the giving thing something besides an exercise in hypocrisy.

"What do you hope your family makes you?" Jennilynn questioned, interrupting my silent reflections.

I laughed sardonically. "Me?" I shook my head. "Nothing," I answered crisply, staring at Jennilynn.

"Nobody's giving me anything. I didn't ever figure they would."

Jennilynn cocked her head to one side. "Everybody gets something."

I was too tired to weave another tale so Jennilynn wouldn't learn the truth about our family's holiday woes. "It doesn't matter anymore." I shrugged wearily. "That's just the way things will be this Christmas. For us, at least."

Jennilynn smiled. "That proves it, just like I said— you're totally unselfish. You do all these things for your family, but you don't care whether you get anything back. I guess that's part of the giving thing, too, isn't it?"

"Jennilynn Lewis, you are *so* weird." I was exasperated. I suppose I was also tired of Jennilynn not being able to see through my sham. "Not everybody's like you and your family." I bit my lower lip, debating whether to make a full confession. I decided that it didn't matter anymore. Sooner or later she'd find out the awful truth, but I suspected that the truth about my family's poverty wouldn't matter much to Jennilynn. "Jen, we don't have any money for Christmas. We're poor." I cleared my throat and stared down at the quilt. "We've been poor ever since my dad's accident. That was before I'd even heard of Eagar, Arizona. That's why we moved here and why we live in Mrs. Thurman's tiny little house. We don't have any money, not for Christmas, not for hardly anything."

Jennilynn stopped working. "Nothing?" she questioned slowly, the shock of my revelation hard for her to grasp.

"Nothing," I admitted with a sigh, avoiding Jennilynn's eyes. "So that's why I made up the giving thing. I don't know what anybody else in my family is doing. Probably nothing." I tried to sound indifferent. I glanced up. The pathetic look on Jennilynn's face made me smile. "Don't worry," I laughed. "It's no big deal. It's not like we're starving or anything. Forget it."

Jennilynn quietly returned to her quilting. I suspected that my candid confession had made her uncomfortable. After a while, she poked her needle into the quilt and looked over at me. The sad, pathetic look was gone from her face. "Nadine, I wish my family was poor too."

"What?" I sputtered. "Why would you wish for something totally dumb like that?"

"Maybe not poor exactly," she responded. "Just . . ." She thought a moment. "What I mean is . . . I'm tired of Christmas out of a store. I like your giving thing better."

I shook my head. "But you're going to have your own TV and stereo. All to yourself, in your very own room. You're going to Disneyland. Those are just the big things. You'll probably get tons of smaller things."

Jennilynn nodded sadly. "Yeah, and I'll be able to go to my room, close the door, and watch the TV and listen to the stereo. All by myself."

"You can invite me over if you get lonely," I offered, grinning.

"Of course I'll want you to come over." She sighed deeply. "But every time you pass your parents' bedroom, it'll be like Christmas all over again, for you and for them. They'll love your quilt tons more than anything you could buy in the store."

I was taken aback because I suddenly realized that what she was saying was true. "*You* could make a quilt too," I offered slowly.

"Christmas is only a week and a half away."

I thought a moment and then declared confidently, "If Wendy and Sister Mercer help, I'll bet we could finish this one tomorrow. It's almost done now. Then we could all start on yours."

Jennilynn's eyes brightened and a huge grin exploded across her face. For the first time since concocting the giving thing, I experienced my first genuinely sincere giving gesture of the Christmas season. And I didn't even feel forced to do it! Right then, more than anything I wanted to help Jennilynn make a quilt. Suddenly I felt a surge of warmth inside me.

Jennilynn's face glowed. "Would you really help me, Nadine?"

"Oh, you big goof," I muttered, trying not to laugh. "Why wouldn't I help you with your quilt after everything you've done for me? We'll make you a gorgeous quilt—a giving quilt." I laughed. "You can't even imagine how great this quilt is going to be!"

"Will it be as nice as this one?" she asked hopefully.

I thought a moment and then teased with a straight face, "I really don't think anybody could make a quilt as beautiful as mine." I grinned wildly. "But we'll make it close enough that your mom and dad won't know the difference."

CHAPTER 7

"And where were the two of you this afternoon?" Mom unexpectedly asked Wendy and me as we were helping her put dinner on the table. "I hardly see you anymore after school."

Mom's question caught me completely unawares. I took a stack of plates to the table and glanced over at Wendy, tacitly soliciting her help. "We were over at Sister Mercer's place," I explained, swallowing slowly.

"Actually," Wendy joined in, taking utensils from the drawer, "we're helping Jennilynn make a Christmas present for her parents."

I nodded. "Yeah, but it's a secret and there's still tons of work to do."

Mom laughed. "Your secret's safe with me."

Just then there was a knock. Garrett headed for the front door. "It's probably Cory," he announced. "He said he was dropping by this evening."

But Garrett didn't open the door to find his friend Cory. Instead, a beaming Marge Thurman stood on the front step wrapped in her elegant fur coat holding the leashes to two medium-size dancing poodles, the one coal black and the other pure white, both wearing matching red-and-gold tailored jackets that gave them a snobbish, royal air.

The two dogs barked and bounded raucously into the living room. Smiling broadly, Mrs. Thurman followed, tugged forward by the high-energy dogs. Mrs. Thurman, usually so stiff, formal, and forbidding, now behaved in a positively ridiculous, giddy fashion. Aghast, I wondered if she had suddenly lost the very last of her mental marbles and was teetering on the brink of lunacy.

Hearing the racket, Dad came from the bedroom and stared in shock as the dogs pattered across the living-room carpet and pranced into the kitchen, where their padded feet and trimmed nails scratched and clicked across the tile floor. Ecstatic, the dogs sniffed the table legs and chairs. I was waiting for one of them to do some dreadfully disgusting thing on the floor while Mrs. Thurman looked on, beaming her approval.

Dad was adamantly opposed to any animal larger than a tiny turtle or a miniature goldfish living under the same roof as the family. To have someone barge into the house with a pair of dogs was more than he could endure. Detecting Dad's impending explosion of protest, Mom put a restraining hand on his shoulder and ordered firmly, "Ted, I'll handle this."

"What do you think?" Mrs. Thurman bubbled, admiring the two poodles that tugged excitedly on their leashes and barked in high-pitched yaps. "Should I let them loose?" she asked, bending over to unsnap the leashes. "They love to run."

"No," Dad boomed, startling the dogs and Mrs. Thurman.

"Since they're in new surroundings, maybe you'd better keep them on their leashes," Mom spoke up, eyeing Dad warningly.

"Aren't they the most adorable things in the whole world?" Mrs. Thurman gushed. "I'm sure the girls will love them—don't you think so?" She was absolutely smitten, although a little exhausted too. I had never seen her exhibit anything but her stern, stilted, high-brow manner, and now she was behaving as though we were her close friends, dying to see her dumb dogs.

I glowered at the animals, unable to disguise my displeasure, but Mrs. Thurman was too enamored with the curly-haired, dancing dogs to notice. "There's our *entire* Christmas," I thought, choking on my bitterness.

"I have a small favor to ask the children." Mrs. Thurman turned to me and then smiled at Garrett. "Until my granddaughters arrive and take the dogs themselves, I need someone to look after them. They need to be fed and bathed. They'll need daily walks. Of course, I'll pay."

"I'm sure Nadine and Garrett would love to take care of the dogs," Mom volunteered.

"I'll give them one dollar each to take care of the dogs between now and Christmas," Mrs. Thurman offered. "They'd probably do it for free," she said, grinning proudly, "but I insist on paying. The dogs are so full of energy." She took a deep breath and added, "But they're wearing me out. They don't ever settle down. It will be nice having someone else walk them and take care of them. I could leave them here with you if you'd like."

"No," Dad spoke up firmly. "Nadine and Garrett can get the dogs at your place."

While my indignation boiled, Mom listened intently to Mrs. Thurman's mindless chatter about the poodles. By the time Mrs. Thurman left, I was bursting with annoyance.

"There's probably poodle hair all over," Dad grumbled as soon as the door closed. "They didn't do anything on the floor, did they?" He made a quick inspection under the table.

"Man, she's got a whole lot of nerve to bring those stupid dogs in here," Garrett growled.

"Garrett," Mom scolded, "there is no call for comments like that. Mrs. Thurman just wanted to share her joy with all of us."

"If she is so interested in sharing," I complained, "why doesn't she share something we actually want?"

"Nadine, you like dogs. You've begged us to get a dog."

"I don't want *those* dogs. Poodles are so snooty and useless, like having a big rat. Why did she think we'd care a hoot about her dogs?"

"Because we're her friends and neighbors," Mom answered softly, sadly.

"Oh, really?" I retorted. "She steals our entire Christmas to buy poodles and then wants us to be excited to see them? And when did we become Mrs. Thurman's friends?"

"I'm her friend," Mom responded quietly, "and I'm glad she brought her dogs over. It shows that she trusts us. Coming to our house was a big step for her. She's opening up. We should be happy about that. I am."

"Well, I sure don't plan to walk her dumb dogs," I murmured. "Not for a measly dollar."

"Then I'll walk them," Mom volunteered. "And I'll do it for nothing."

Garrett and I did finally agree to take care of Mrs. Thurman's dogs, but we tried our hardest not to be happy about it. That same evening he and I were on dish duty. To pass the time we mischievously concocted imaginary disasters that might befall Mrs. Thurman's dogs.

"We can always walk them past Bill Parker's place," Garrett suggested. "His big German shepherd looks pretty hungry about four o'clock every afternoon. Of course, he'd end up with one gigantic hair ball after eating one of those poodles."

"Maybe we could kidnap them and write a ransom note," I giggled. "We'll demand that she give us back our Christmas money."

"You know, it really would be too bad if we took them for a walk and they accidentally slipped out of their collars and were never seen again." Garrett howled with laughter.

The next day after school, as soon as I walked through the front door, the phone rang. It was Mrs. Thurman. She was calling to remind me to take the poodles for their daily walk. I had planned to help Jennilynn with her quilt, but Mom insisted that I walk the dogs first. When I called Jennilynn to tell her the bad news, I was surprised that she wasn't at all disappointed. "Can I help?" she pleaded. "Please."

"They're darling," Jennilynn laughed when Mrs. Thurman turned the dogs over to us. "I love their little wool walking jackets and their permed coats," she exclaimed.

"They're really ready for a walk," Mrs. Thurman sighed. "I almost broke down and took them myself. I locked them in the garage, and they howled and yapped most of the afternoon."

Jennilynn and I started down Mrs. Thurman's driveway, each of us clasping a leash. "I feel like a rich, high-society lady," Jennilynn laughed as her dog tugged her along.

ALMA J. YATES

"I feel like a servant," I muttered, glaring irritably at my dog. "Mrs. Thurman's granddaughters probably won't even want these stupid dogs."

"Of course they will," Jennilynn came back. "Why wouldn't they?"

"What are they going to do with two yapping dogs in the middle of Boston?"

"The same thing that we're doing with them in Eagar." Jennilynn beamed. "I wish they were mine."

I couldn't quite understand why Jennilynn was so annoyingly enthusiastic when it came to taking care of Marge Thurman's poodles. To me the dogs were a terrible reminder of how every penny of our Christmas money had been squandered by Mrs. Thurman. I found it extremely difficult to forgive her for that.

* * *

The week prior to Christmas was a frantic blur as I rushed to finish my gifts and help Jennilynn with her quilt. Jennilynn grew ecstatic as she watched the quilt change from a bundle of batting and yards of folded fabric into the charming quilt that was destined to grace her parents' bed. "It's the most beautiful thing in the whole world," she gushed dramatically, running her hands across the taut cloth as it lay stretched on Sister Mercer's quilting frames. "It *is* pretty, isn't it, Sister Mercer?" she prodded.

Sister Mercer laughed. "Jennilynn, I wish it were mine," she kindly reassured her.

"Don't you just love it, Nadine?" she exclaimed, begging my approval for seemingly the hundredth time.

"Of course it's nice," I teased, fighting back a grin. I couldn't help adding, "Though not nearly as nice as mine." I burst out laughing when I saw Jennilynn's worried frown. "But, Jen," I quickly added to allay her fears, "if I didn't have mine, yours would be my next choice. Besides, your mom and dad probably won't ever see my quilt so they'll never know that they ended up with the second-best quilt in the world."

"Oh, I didn't mean that yours wasn't beautiful too," Jennilynn amended. Wendy and Sister Mercer laughed as they watched our playful exchange, one that had become common as all of us had worked feverishly to complete Jennilynn's quilt. "It's so much better than anything I could buy, even if I had a million dollars. Mom and Dad will love it, don't you think?"

"Oh, don't be so wacky." I grinned, shaking my head. "Of course, they'll love it." I couldn't help tossing out another mischievous barb. "But, Jen, they'd love it even if it was an old, ratty rag."

"But it's not an old, ratty rag!" Jennilynn protested.

"Don't let Nadine tease you, Jen," Wendy giggled.

Jennilynn's face exploded into a beatific smile. "I can hardly wait till Christmas. It'll be my best one ever."

I laughed at Jennilynn and envied her, not because of her TV, stereo, and trip to Disneyland, but because she had somehow taken the giving thing, wrapped it in her own innocent heart, and transformed her Christmas into the most wonderful holiday of her life. I hoped that I could find that same magic.

The week of Christmas was filled with parties and programs. Christmas music and decorations were everywhere. Dad and Daniel had made Marge Thurman's place a magical Christmas fantasy. There were literally thousands of lights strung about. A life-size Santa was perched on the roof and a small manger scene sat on the front lawn. There wasn't another house in all of Eagar so beautifully decorated.

A few days before Christmas I sneaked home from Sister Mercer's place with my Christmas quilt folded neatly inside a large plastic garbage bag. No one saw me slip into the house. Surreptitiously I closed my bedroom door and spread the quilt on my own bed, just to get a good look at it. It seemed such a perfect fit, maybe a little big on my twin bed, but that just meant that there was more of it to wrap snugly around me.

For a long time I admired it, then cautiously, almost furtively, I lay on my bed and snuggled slowly into the quilt. The soft flannel felt wonderful against my skin, and the smell of the fresh, new material filled my nose. Suddenly, and entirely unexpectedly, I fell in love with this beautiful quilt. I imagined myself going to bed each night and burrowing under the quilt's puffy, soft warmth.

Suddenly the door burst open and Wendy barged into the room. I leaped guiltily from the quilt. In my wild scramble I bashed my knee into the dresser.

"Are you all right?" Wendy inquired with a grin, tossing her coat onto her bed as I dropped to the floor and clutched my throbbing knee. "I didn't mean to scare you."

I grimaced, getting up and folding the quilt. "I just wasn't expecting anyone."

"Hey," Wendy called out, grabbing my arm, "let me see what it looks like on the bed." I spread it out again for Wendy's benefit. She whistled appreciatively as she reached out and touched the quilt. "I love it." She gathered the quilt in her arms and spread it out on her bed. Stepping back a few feet, she admired it. "Now, Nadine, that's where it looks really nice," she joked. "Since you probably don't have a present for me, give me the quilt and find something else for Mom and Dad. They won't know the difference. After all, I am your favorite sister."

"For your information, I already have something for you."

"Give Mom and Dad my gift." She smiled and raised her eyebrows in quick succession. "You won't even have to wrap it. Just leave it on my bed starting right now." She grinned.

"Very funny," I grumbled as I began folding the quilt again. "I've been doing some thinking, though," I said, making certain that I didn't look directly at Wendy. "I made a 3-D manger scene in school for Mom and Dad. It turned out really nice."

Wendy laughed again. "Well, since they've got a Christmas present, I'll keep the quilt."

For a moment I stood there, my mind suddenly latching on to Wendy's facetious remark, but twisting it just enough that I could see a door of opportunity open a crack. A wicked wad of selfishness expanded inside me, and I wondered if I really wanted to give my quilt away. After all, the quilt might be the only really special gift I'd receive this Christmas.

"I do have a gift for Mom and Dad," I said slowly, my mind trying to rationalize my next move. "I mean, I worked really hard on the manger. Miss Elkins said mine was the best one in the whole class." I coughed. "So I've been wondering if maybe . . ." I gulped before blurting out the final words. "Maybe I should just keep the quilt." The smile drooped from Wendy's face. "Mom and Dad won't care," I argued defiantly. "They have tons of blankets. What's one more blanket to them?"

Wendy shrugged. "It's your quilt." She studied me oddly. "But I thought you were making it for Mom and Dad." She shook her head. "That's why I helped you."

"So you wouldn't have helped if you'd known it was just for me?"

Wendy hesitated. "I didn't say that. Not exactly." She quickly shook her head. "I guess you can do anything you want with it, Nadine." After a moment's pause, she added with a smirk, biting down on her lower lip, "You're not going to pull a Marge Thurman, are you?"

"I'm not a bit like Marge Thurman!" I bristled.

"You're not as rich as Marge," Wendy came back with a shrug of her shoulders. She pursed her lips and finished, "But of course you don't have to be rich to be selfish." She laughed and gave me a quick, playful shove and then slipped from the room before I could say more.

That night I called Jennilynn and she told me that she was sure her quilt would be finished before Christmas. She could hardly contain her jubilation. "I know your quilt is beautiful and everything, Nadine, but I can't think of anything in my whole life that I've ever had that I've loved this much."

"Do you think you might want to keep it?" I ventured, hoping I wasn't a terrible person for wanting to keep my quilt.

"What do you mean, keep it?" Jennilynn asked, sounding confused.

"I just mean that maybe you ought to keep it. For yourself."

"And not give it to Mom and Dad?" Jennilynn sounded shocked.

"Well, you really like it, don't you?"

"But I like it so much because I'm giving it to them!"

"Don't they have a nice electric blanket?"

"Sure, they've got an electric blanket, but nothing like my quilt. Besides," she added, perking up, "if I kept it, what would happen to the giving thing? There wouldn't be a giving thing anymore. Everything would just turn into the usual old, ugly *getting* thing."

"And what's wrong with *getting* something for Christmas?" I argued defensively.

"But, Nadine, I've been doing the getting thing all my life. Every year I've gotten lots of things, great things, expensive things, and I hardly remember what any of those things are now. But the getting thing isn't ever as nice as the giving thing. That's why you've made this Christmas better than all the others packed together. You showed me the giving thing."

"Well, I've never gotten as much as you," I grumbled, "so I'm thinking that it's time that I got something, something like my quilt. I made the manger display for Mom and Dad. I didn't buy that, so I'm still sort of doing the giving thing. But I'm getting something, too."

"Maybe that will work just fine for you," Jennilynn said slowly. "You should know. After all, you're the one that came up with the giving thing in the first place."

As I hung up the phone, I knew I hadn't been the one to come up with the giving thing, not the real giving thing, the giving thing that could fill a person with the wonder, thrill, and happiness that Jennilynn was experiencing. I had talked emptily about that giving thing, but a knowing voice nagged inside my head, assuring me that in spite of all my talk and planning, I still hadn't discovered the real secret of the giving thing.

CHAPTER 8

One night shortly before Christmas, as our family gathered in the evening to sing carols and to share Christmas stories, there was a soft knock at the door. Wendy opened it. Marge Thurman stood there in her long fur coat. "May I come in?" she asked meekly.

Wendy stepped aside, and Marge shuffled in. Mom greeted her and took her coat, and Dad surrendered his favorite chair while the rest of us stared without speaking, dreading to discover the purpose of this unexpected intrusion. It seemed Mrs. Thurman always brought bad news. There was no reason to believe that her visit would end any differently.

"I stepped out into the yard to take another look at my Christmas lights, and I heard you singing," she confessed quietly, seeming a bit embarrassed and fidgeting in Dad's chair. "I wanted to come over, but I wasn't sure if I should." She smiled wanly. "Willard loved to sing Christmas carols. He had a beautiful voice." She shook her head disappointedly. "I don't sing well, but I loved to listen to Willard." She clasped her hands in her lap. "When I heard your beautiful voices, I had to come over. I apologize for intruding without an invitation."

"Mrs. Thurman," Mom responded warmly, "you don't need an invitation. You're always welcome. We were just having our family home evening," she explained cheerily.

"Family home evening?" Mrs. Thurman spoke as though she were trying out the phrase for the first time. "That's something you Mormons do, isn't it?" Before Mom could answer, Marge rambled on, blinking a few times. "Willard would have liked your home family evenings." A weak smile played on her lips. "He would have liked a lot of your Mormon customs." She wagged her head wearily. "I wish we had done something like that when our son Robert was growing up." She caught herself and pressed her thin lips together. "But that's all past. Lost opportunities."

"Won't you be seeing your son soon?" Dad inquired soothingly, trying to brighten Marge's melancholy mood. "He should be flying in anytime, shouldn't he?"

Mrs. Thurman cast Dad a strange look as though she weren't sure what he had said. Finally she looked away. Everyone was awkwardly quiet, then Marge commented matter-of-factly, turning to Garrett and me,

"I sent those horrible dogs back this afternoon. The gentleman from the pet store made a special trip to pick them up." She chortled softly, though plaintively. "Such a terrible nuisance those dogs were. My house will never be the same. They almost drove me crazy." She leaned her head back and sighed, "Whatever provoked me to think of poodles?"

She stiffened and a hardness showed in her gaze. "The man at the pet shop wouldn't return all my money," she grumbled, not attempting to disguise the irritation in her tone. "After he agreed to drive to Eagar to pick them up— and he almost didn't do that—he gave me only fifty dollars for both of them. He claimed it was too close to Christmas to sell them. I paid three times that for them." She sighed. "But I guess I'm glad to be rid of them."

"So what are your granddaughters getting for Christmas?" Garrett questioned bluntly. Mom glowered at him, but Garrett merely shrugged and waited for Mrs. Thurman's reply.

"Oh, they'll have lots of nice things. They always do. Robert and his wife spoil them. I would too if they visited more often, but . . ." Her words trailed off into a whisper of sadness.

"Are you ready for them?" Wendy asked kindly. "What fun things do you plan to do?"

Mrs. Thurman closed her eyes for a moment and swallowed hard. "They won't be here for Christmas."

"Did something come up?" Mom asked, sounding both puzzled and worried.

"Deep down I think I suspected it all along. It was fun to imagine, though. I liked thinking about them having Christmas with me." She squinted slightly. "I really think you're the ones that made me really hope they'd come. I'd look across the street and see all of you together, and I just hoped that Robert and his family could join me so that we'd be a happy family like yours. And, of course, all the preparation was so rewarding because it gave me something to do." She glanced at Mom. "You made it enjoyable, Mrs. Cluff. I looked forward to your coming each day. I'm sorry all of your hard work was wasted." She shook her head. "Even when I realized that Robert and his family wouldn't be coming, I didn't want you to stop helping me."

"Will Robert and his family come after Christmas?" Mom wanted to know.

"Robert and his family are going on a little cruise." Mrs. Thurman attempted a smile but failed. "Ten days," she added, her voice trailing off. She looked as though she might cry.

"They're not coming at all?" Mom questioned, her surprise evident.

"I spoke to Robert this morning. They leave the day after Christmas."

"He didn't tell you till this morning?" Dad asked.

"Oh, they didn't exactly . . ." Mrs. Thurman took a white handkerchief from up her sleeve and began twisting and wadding it. "They never actually said they were coming. Not for sure. Last summer they were supposed to drive down this way for a quick visit on their way to Jackson Hole and Yellowstone. They ended up flying to Salt Lake and then taking a rental car north from there. They didn't ever make it down this far, but at that time Robert said they might come for Christmas. We talked about some of the things that we could do during the holiday." She shook her head slowly. "I suppose I shouldn't have gotten my hopes up."

"I don't understand," Mom murmured.

"It was really all my fault." Mrs. Thurman smiled sadly. "I made some rather bold assumptions that I really shouldn't have made." She brightened momentarily. "This morning Robert did say he was flying to Phoenix on business at the end of February. He wants me to meet him in Scottsdale at my home there." She shook her head. "I just kept hoping that maybe the whole family would come for Christmas." She touched her handkerchief to the corner of her eye. "I told myself that he was planning to surprise me. I guess he wasn't." She breathed in deeply and began to ramble some. "I suppose I could have flown to Boston. Robert invited me in a way—saying I could fly out if I wanted to." She shook her head sadly. "But I don't like Boston, especially not in the wintertime."

"But," Wendy burst out, "didn't you tell him about all the stuff you've done—the decorations, the food, and the dogs? I mean, I'll bet if he had known about . . ." Her voice faded.

Mrs. Thurman laughed, but the sound was merely an attempt to disguise the cry that threatened. "They don't want to spend Christmas way out here. Nothing we could have done would have compared to a ten-day cruise. And the dogs . . . well, the dogs were always a very bad idea. I realized that five minutes after they arrived."

"So what will you do for Christmas?" Wendy asked gently.

"I think I'll drive to Scottsdale and spend the holiday there. I should have planned to do that from the very beginning."

* * *

"It just doesn't seem right," Wendy remarked as we gathered around the kitchen table munching popcorn and sipping hot chocolate after Mrs. Thurman had slipped into the night, a sad shadow drifting off to her lonely home. Mom had invited her to stay for refreshments, but she'd declined.

Mom heaved a sigh. "And what will Marge do with all that food she loaded in her freezer and cupboards? I've helped her buy so much because she wanted her family to have such nice things. She can't possibly use all that food herself." Mom shook her head. "My heart just aches for her."

"I can't believe her son won't come for Christmas," Wendy lamented.

"Actually," Garrett spoke up, fighting back a grin, "I can believe it. I'm not sure I'd want to spend my Christmas with Mrs. Thurman. Would you?"

"Garrett," Dad said loudly in reprimand, "there will be no comments like that."

There was a part of me that agreed with Garrett's flippant remark. Ever since realizing that Mrs. Thurman was never going to share her abundance with us, and especially since she had taken our Christmas money, I had harbored ill feelings toward her. Even though my heart was softened some after witnessing Mrs. Thurman's dismal dilemma, there was still a part of me that derived a certain cruel satisfaction in knowing that our neighbor was getting what she deserved.

That night I tossed anxiously in the midst of a strange, disconcerting dream where I furtively followed Marge Thurman through the streets of Eagar, doing everything in my power to stay hidden—slipping behind fences, bushes, and trees, and peering around the corners of houses. Suddenly I found myself in the cemetery, just like I had been the first day that I'd followed her. She shuffled awkwardly to Willard's grave and sat hunched on the ground in front of the headstone, her back to me, a dark picture of misery and woe. I crept closer until I was hidden behind a headstone only a few short feet from where Mrs. Thurman wept silently.

Once again I found myself deriving a certain morbid, cruel satisfaction from this pitiful picture. I smugly considered how totally selfish she was. I thought of how she had callously stolen our money, money we so desperately needed to celebrate our own simple Christmas. I thought of the poodles Mrs. Thurman had so foolishly purchased. I found myself becoming angry and resentful, and glad that Mrs. Thurman would spend her holiday lonely and sad. It was in the midst of those harsh, heartless sentiments that Mrs. Thurman slowly turned and stared in my direction. I shrank back in sur- prised horror because I was staring straight into Mrs. Thurman's face, but the face wasn't Mrs. Thurman's. It was my young face locked inside Mrs. Thurman's bent and aged body.

I gasped in my sleep and sat bolt upright in bed. It was night and I could hear Wendy's heavy breathing across the room, so I knew the dream was over, but I was still trembling from the shock of seeing my own face. I clenched my fists and shook my head. I wasn't like Mrs. Thurman. I wasn't cold and selfish, I insisted. I was doing the giving thing, I argued. I had made gifts for everyone in the family, and I probably wasn't getting anything in return. But I shuddered, knowing full well that I couldn't possibly lie to myself. I knew that I had only *pretended* to do the giving thing, simply to hide our family's shameful poverty. I wasn't giving to truly give. I was a hypocrite, and my gifts were just something to hide behind.

The next morning I thought about each of my gifts, and I desperately willed myself to give each one with a sincere, generous heart. I didn't want to be a fake any longer. I didn't want to merely go through the outward motions. I wanted to be genuine. I wanted to erase every shred of selfishness from my heart because I suspected that if I didn't, somehow through the years I would evolve into a person just like Marge Thurman, a woman withered and warped with selfishness. I shuddered, contemplating that horrible thought.

The last day of school before Christmas break, Jennilynn and I had volunteered to help Miss Elkins clean her classroom. Our offer turned into more of a project than either of us had anticipated because Miss Elkins also wanted to take down all her bulletin boards and Christmas decorations. She had used yards of colorful holiday wrapping paper as the background for her boards. I asked her if she planned to keep the wrapping paper for the following year's decorations.

"No," Miss Elkins replied tiredly, "just throw it away."

"May I keep it?" I asked hesitantly, hopefully.

"Some of it's wrinkled," Miss Elkins pointed out.

"That won't matter," I assured her.

Miss Elkins's giftwrap was an unexpected luxury, and I used it to wrap all of my presents. Delicately, I placed Wendy's dry arrangement in a big box so as not to crush or damage it; then I wrapped the box. The boys' gym bags were next, followed by Daniel's family portrait. I carefully wrapped the manger scene, making certain that I used the very best wrapping paper. There was even enough paper to cover Mom and Dad's huge, puffy quilt. On a white card that I taped to the side of the gift-wrapped quilt, I wrote in big, bold letters, "To Mom and Dad, from Nadine." Although just a few days earlier I had coveted my own quilt, the memory of my dream burned painfully in my mind, and more than anything I wanted Mom and Dad to have the quilt.

Our Christmas tree, an unexpected gift from a neighbor down the street, had been rather bare underneath, a blunt reminder to all of us that this was going to be a poor family's Christmas. As soon as my gifts were wrapped, I arranged them invitingly beneath the spreading branches of the squat, bushy fir tree, hoping to ignite a bit of Christmas cheer.

At breakfast Dad commented jovially, glancing toward the tree, "I see that Santa's already made a surprise appearance. And I didn't think we were going to have any gifts this Christmas."

Mom smiled warmly in my direction and commented brightly, "Nadine has been busy. She's a regular Christmas elf."

I felt myself blush. "Don't get your hopes up," I muttered. "It's just junk I made myself. There's really not much to it."

"I don't know about anybody else," Dad teased with a twinkle in his eyes, "but I can hardly wait to see what kind of junk you've made for me."

"Dad," I grumbled, feeling embarrassed and guilty all at the same time, "junk is junk wherever it comes from."

That afternoon Mom sent me outside to take a bag of garbage to the trash can at the corner of our house. A cold, blustery wind, filled with a few swirling sprinkles of snow, blew fiercely, pulling at my hair. Just as I dumped the trash, Mrs. Thurman's Cadillac turned from the street and drove slowly up her long driveway. Even though I was cold without a coat on, I watched her curiously.

Before Mrs. Thurman pulled into her garage, she stopped the car and stepped out to pick up the town newspaper from her lawn. As soon as she stepped from the car, a howling gust of wind huffed harshly across her yard, whipping her skirt and coat. The force of the gust caused her to stagger and turn back to her car, and as she did, several sheets of paper flew from her open car door and went sliding and tumbling across the lawn in a twirling, choppy invisible wave of air, headed straight for the street.

Mrs. Thurman screamed, and with both arms thrust out as though she might snatch the papers before they disappeared in the winter gale, she started after them, but it became painfully clear that she was not agile enough to make the chase.

At first I found the whole scene rather comical, but then I was running. I'm not sure why. It was as though something bigger and stronger than me pressed me into service, and I decided to chase down the fluttering papers that had now blown into the street.

Within moments I'd snatched up the first three sheets of paper. The next two were more elusive, careening and skidding down the pavement in a teasing game of keep-away, but I finally overtook them when they blew into Mr. Rogers's rosebushes. The final sheet of paper seemed to have disappeared altogether, but I continued down the street another block hoping that I would see it. Shivering in my T-shirt with the wind howling about me, I was about to return home when I spotted a lone sheet of white paper flapping against Mr. Hollingsworth's backyard fence. Slipping into his yard, I grabbed the paper, which looked similar to the other five I already had. With the six sheets of paper in hand, I headed back to Mrs. Thurman's house against the wind's icy, tearing blasts.

By the time I reached Mrs. Thurman's driveway, the Cadillac was in the garage. With my arms covered with goose bumps, I stepped to the giant oak door and rang the bell. Immediately the door opened, and Mrs. Thurman stood there, still in her long, black coat, her face a pale gray, her eyes wide and frantic.

"I found your papers," I announced, my teeth chattering slightly.

"Come in, girl," she burst out, motioning me inside. "Come out of that dreadful wind."

I stepped in and Mrs. Thurman closed the door behind me. "I think I got them all," I explained, handing her the papers. "I only saw six fly away."

Mrs. Thurman took the papers and pressed them to her breast. "I thought they were gone for sure," she whispered with her eyes closed. "They are terribly important. They are for some property I own. I shouldn't have left them lying loose like that on the seat. I don't know what I would have done had I lost them." She opened her eyes and stared at me. "I saw you run down the street, but I was afraid to even hope that you were really going after my papers, and even if you were, I didn't think it was possible for you to ever find them all, not in this horrible wind."

Her shoulders sagged and she appeared as though she might actually collapse right there in the entryway. She swallowed and took in a deep breath. "I prayed." She shook her head. "And I'm not a praying woman, but when those papers blew away, I prayed with all my heart." She gulped. "I hardly dared believe that any prayer of mine could ever be answered, but, young lady, you're an answer to my prayers."

She stiffened as though something had suddenly occurred to her. Turning, she lunged toward the credenza. Setting the papers down, she snatched her purse, opened it and dug inside for a moment. When she finally turned, she held two bills, one in each hand, a one and a five. For a moment she studied them both as though debating, and then in a surprise gesture, she thrust the five-dollar bill in front of me. "Take it!" she rasped, wetting her thin lips. "I want you to have it for retrieving my papers."

Her unexpected, overly generous offer startled me. No one had ever paid me five dollars for anything. But I couldn't take the money. And the truly strange phenomenon was that I didn't even want it, and yet, I should have wanted it. I should have been wildly grateful for it, but I wasn't. Slowly I shook my head. "I didn't do it for money," I responded quietly.

"But you have to take it," she pleaded. "I want you to take it. You have no idea how important those papers are. Please!"

I shook my head again. "I'd feel kind of dumb taking your money after being an answer to your prayer." I smiled, suddenly feeling warm and wonderful. It was as though something soothing melted inside me and moved outward, driving away all the chill that I had been feeling.

"I don't know that I've ever been an answer to some-body's prayer. I don't think you're supposed to get paid for answering prayers. Not with money," I added quietly.

Mrs. Thurman held the money out farther. "Then take it for . . ." She shook her head in utter confusion. "Take it for cleaning my yard. You did such a beautiful job on my yard a few weeks ago."

I laughed, strangely enjoying this unique exchange. "But you already paid me for that, remember?"

"But I didn't pay you very much, hardly anything at all. I should have paid you more. After I sent you away, I felt guilty for being so stingy. This can make up for that."

Instinctively, I knew there was no way that I could take Mrs. Thurman's money. I knew if I did, anything good that I had just felt would somehow vanish and I would never recapture it. "I'm glad I found your papers," I said, backing toward the door. "And I'm glad I could be an answer to your prayer." I turned and slipped out the front door.

For a moment I stood on Mrs. Thurman's front step and stared out across her huge yard. The cold, blustery wind was still blowing, but it didn't chill me as it had moments before. The late afternoon sun peeked momentarily from behind a bank of gray, churning clouds, and I thought I saw something sparkle to my right. I glanced in that direction, and there in the dirt surrounding a small, green shrub, I saw a single coin. A nickel. I suspected that it was one that I had thrown there weeks earlier. Smiling, I crept over to the shrub and snatched up the coin. Clutching it in my hand, I returned home.

ALMA J. YATES

CHAPTER 9

Mom roused the family early Christmas Eve morning because it was a family tradition to spend the day making goody plates for neighbors and friends. Our little kitchen was quickly transformed into a whirlwind of holiday activity as everyone, even Dad, made rolls, pies, cookies, candies, and popcorn balls. In the midst of the cooking and baking, laughing and talking, teasing and joking, I forgot about being poor this Christmas.

The day whipped past as we cooked, baked, and delivered plates of goodies around the neighborhood. By late afternoon we'd cleaned up and prepared a light supper of chicken noodle soup and Mom's hot rolls. After supper we planned to hold our traditional Christmas Eve program—reading the Christmas story from Luke and Matthew, singing carols, telling stories, and hanging out the Christmas stockings.

"I invited Mrs. Thurman to join us tonight," Mom remarked casually as she put a pan of white, puffy rolls into the oven.

"I thought she was going to Scottsdale," Wendy commented, wiping off the kitchen counter.

"A storm is blowing in," Mom replied, closing the oven door. "If she goes, it won't be till later."

"She isn't coming, is she?" Garrett grumbled. "That would ruin everything."

It surprised me that Mom didn't scold him. Instead she took a deep breath and looked about the kitchen. "No one should spend Christmas alone."

"But Mrs. Thurman is . . ." Garrett didn't finish his sentence. He merely scowled and shook his head as he set the chairs around the kitchen table.

"She'll be here in a few minutes," Mom went on. "Let's make her feel welcome."

"Who has to sit by her?" Garrett complained.

"Whoever would like to," Mom replied simply.

A few moments later, I shuffled down the hall to my room. My feelings toward Mrs. Thurman had changed during the last two days. I didn't despise her as I had done earlier. I began combing my hair in the mirror above the dresser, and as I pulled the comb through my hair, I spotted a lone nickel, the one that I had picked up from Mrs. Thurman's yard the day before. I thought about the forty-nine cents I had earned for cleaning

Mrs. Thurman's huge yard. I contrasted those measly coins with the five-dollar bill I could have received for merely retrieving a few papers blowing in the wind. I recalled how angry I had been when Mrs. Thurman had given me the forty-nine cents; I had expected so much more. On the other hand, I hadn't expected anything when she had thrust the five-dollar bill toward me, insisting that I take it. I smiled, pondering the prayer Mrs. Thurman had offered, a prayer that I had unknowingly been able to answer. I was grateful that I had declined her money. And I realized that I was finally beginning to understand what Mom had tried to teach me a few weeks earlier when she'd explained that Christmas didn't have anything to do with money and giving material things. Instead it had everything to do with giving something of yourself.

I picked up the nickel and felt its coolness in the palm of my hand, and as I did I wondered if Mrs. Thurman had been praying again today, praying for someone to care about her, praying for a place to stay, praying that she wouldn't be lonely on this most special of all nights of the year.

I clutched the nickel tightly in my fist. I couldn't help thinking of another cold, dark night two thousand years ago when someone else had no place to go and was turned away from every inn. They'd had to settle for a lowly stable. I smiled to think our little house was kind of like a lowly stable compared to some. I wondered if Mary had prayed for someone to rescue her and her soon-to-be-born child. I felt a melting in my heart as I considered the tiny baby lying in a lonely manger, the baby who would eventually grow to be a man and teach the whole world about the true giving thing, the giving thing that had absolutely nothing to do with money and stuff.

I swallowed, feeling the burn of tears in my eyes. I thought of *my* giving thing, fraught with fraud, that strange plan that I had concocted in a desperate attempt to hide my own shame, and I realized that for me, at least in the beginning, the giving thing had never been about giving; it had been all about my getting. But I had finally discovered that the more I gave, sincerely gave, the more genuine joy I felt. And, ironically, I also discovered that my desire for getting something back had radically diminished with each attempt to give.

Bursting into the kitchen while pulling on my coat, I called out, "I'll go get Mrs. Thurman so she won't have to come alone."

Garrett and Wendy stared strangely in my direction. "She only lives across the street," Garrett groaned. "Don't you think she can find us on her own?"

"I think that would be very nice, Nadine," Mom responded.

I rushed across the street and up the long driveway, hoping that I would reach Mrs. Thurman before she started out her door. I didn't want her to come alone, and as I hurried up the driveway, I felt a burst of warmth inside me.

I rang the doorbell and waited. Slowly, noiselessly, the front door opened, and there stood Mrs. Thurman, dressed in a long, red dress with a white scarf about her neck. It was the first time I had seen her in anything but black. She seemed surprised to see me, but she motioned for me to come in.

"You look nice, Mrs. Thurman," I complimented her, smiling. "You look all ready for Christmas. I came for you."

Mrs. Thurman gave me a wan, tenuous smile. "I was just getting ready to call. I had decided not to go."

"Not go?" I questioned, perplexed. I glanced around the entryway and spotted Mrs. Thurman's coat on the credenza next to a package. "But supper's almost ready. We've got a place set for you. You've got to come."

Mrs. Thurman shook her head. "It's Christmas Eve. Your family should celebrate together. You shouldn't have to worry about intruders. I think I should just stay here."

"Not on Christmas Eve," I burst out. "Not alone. We're waiting for you. We want you to come." I hesitated and then hastily added, "*I* want you to come. Please, Mrs. Thurman!" Stepping to the credenza, I picked up Mrs. Thurman's coat and held it up so she could slip it on.

Mrs. Thurman smiled and shook her head. "I just don't know if I should."

An idea suddenly burst inside my mind. "Of course you should. You know you should. That's why you prayed me here again. Just like yesterday."

Mrs. Thurman's eyes widened in surprise. "How did you know that?" she whispered, sounding truly shocked. "How did you know I prayed for you again?" She smiled cautiously. "You're the one I hoped would come. How did you possibly know that I had prayed for you?" she rasped.

I smiled and shook my head. "I didn't," I returned quietly. "But He did. He just sent me. You see, Mrs. Thurman, I guess He doesn't want you spending Christmas alone."

CHAPTER 10

The rest of the family was gathered around the kitchen table when Mrs. Thurman and I entered. I took her coat and hung it in the hall closet while Mom led her to a place at the table. As Mrs. Thurman approached the table, she stopped and held up her hand. "I almost forgot," she said, forcing an uncertain smile. She held up the brown package she was carrying. Quickly she tore off the brown paper and extracted a silver-and-gold tin. "I brought a fruitcake," she exclaimed, holding up the tin, which was polished and decorated with pressed Christmas designs. "Willard always had a Christmas fruitcake that he ordered from a place in Wisconsin." She sighed, shaking her head. "I'm carrying on the Christmas tradition." She held the tin as though debating. Finally she held it out toward Mom. "I want your family to have it. It's a five-pound cake," she proclaimed proudly.

Smiling, Mom remarked, "We haven't had a fruitcake for a long time."

Embarrassed for Mrs. Thurman, I looked at the floor, knowing full well why it had been so long since we'd had fruitcake—Dad was the only one who could stand the stuff, and even then just a tiny piece washed down with lots of milk. I knew that of all the gifts Mrs. Thurman could afford to give, fruitcake was the least likely to be appreciated by our family. I wondered silently how long that cake would molder in the cupboard before someone in total exasperation finally wrapped it in newspaper and stuffed it in the garbage can.

"I never had much use for fruitcake," Mrs. Thurman remarked unexpectedly, tainting the genuineness of her gift. She laughed and shook her head. "I could never quite understand why Willard liked the loathsome stuff. But this is a very expensive one." She nodded her head. "It cost almost fifteen dollars."

Mom asked Wendy to take Mrs. Thurman's gift. "I love the container," Wendy exclaimed politely, trying to say something positive. Gently she ran her fingers over the intricately embossed silver-and-gold cake tin.

"Oh, if you don't mind," Mrs. Thurman quickly added, "I'd like the tin back when you've eaten the fruitcake. I collect them. Willard ate the cakes, and I saved the tins."

"It will be our special Christmas treat," Mom said graciously.

At any other time Mrs. Thurman's blind, insensitive selfishness might have caused me to mumble unkindly under my breath, but on this night I felt only sad pity for her, and all the while I hoped desperately that the rest of the family wouldn't notice Mrs. Thurman's obvious flaw.

The family silently and awkwardly began taking their places around the table. I realized immediately that everyone was looking for a spot away from Mrs. Thurman. "I'll sit by Mrs. Thurman," I volunteered, stepping to the chair next to Marge.

Mrs. Thurman laughed. "There isn't anybody I'd rather have sit by me, young lady," she said, dropping onto her own chair. She reached up and squeezed my hand.

Avoiding everybody else's questioning gaze, I slipped into the chair next to Marge. Looking down at her place setting, I noticed a chipped soup bowl. Snatching the imperfect bowl, I exclaimed, "Yours is chipped. I'll take it."

As soon as the blessing was said, I took Mrs. Thurman's bowl and served her some chicken noodle soup. Throughout the meal I checked to make certain she had rolls and butter, a second serving of soup, more milk, another napkin. I listened attentively as she talked almost nonstop about her husband Willard. Desperately, I wanted her to feel comfortable on this special night because I truly wanted to be an answer to her prayer. Never in my life had I felt so impelled to help someone.

It was as though something was pressing me into service. But I wasn't being pressed into service unwillingly. I wanted to reach out to Marge Thurman. I wanted to help her because I suddenly feared that if I didn't, quite possibly no one else would.

When it was time to clear the table and wash the dishes, Mom invited me to take Mrs. Thurman to the sofa in the living room. Wendy and Garrett glared at me, probably assuming that my solicitous manner was a furtive, underhanded ploy to escape kitchen duty.

As soon as the dishes were washed and the kitchen was cleaned, the family gathered in the living room. I sat next to Mrs. Thurman, wanting more than anything to protect her, to somehow shield her from loneliness. I thought of Willard Thurman, whom I'd never met, and I sensed that he was watching me and hoping that I would watch after his lonely wife. I didn't want to disappoint him.

We sang "Far, Far Away on Judea's Plains" and followed that with "I Heard the Bells on Christmas Day." Dad read from Luke and Matthew and then the family sang "O Little Town of Bethlehem" and "While Shepherds Watched Their Flocks." We closed with "Silent Night," and then Mom and Dad both told Christmas stories from their youth.

Mrs. Thurman was silent throughout the entire program. Twice I saw her dab at tears in the corners of her eyes.

As Mom told of a special Christmas she'd had when she was only nine, Mrs. Thurman reached out and took my hand. I sensed that she wasn't fully aware that she had taken it. She clasped my hand between both of hers and held it in her lap while she listened intently to Mom's Christmas story.

"Perhaps Mrs. Thurman would like to share one of her favorite Christmases?" Dad suggested unexpectedly when Mom had finished.

Mrs. Thurman smiled and looked around. "This has been such a lovely evening," she said, her voice cracking with emotion. "I'm glad I didn't go to Scottsdale. This is so much better." She took a deep breath and bit down on her lower lip. "I was just thinking of . . ." Smiling, she shook her head. "As I've sat here with all of you, I have been thinking of Willard, wishing he were here." She closed her eyes momentarily. "I almost feel that part of him is here tonight. You would have all liked Willard. Everybody did. Willard was funny. It took so little to make him happy. He used to joke that when he was growing up, his family was so poor he was ecstatic if he found an orange in his stocking Christmas morning." She chuckled ruefully. "He claimed that he didn't even care if it was a bit soft and had a patch of blue, hairy mold on it."

Marge heaved a heavy sigh. "Until I married Willard, I didn't ever know what it was like to go without. Mine was a rather wealthy family, so I didn't worry about having things. Everything was always just there. I was terribly shy, though. I had private tutors, and I preferred to shut myself up and play the piano or the flute or read books. I read literally hundreds of books.

"The first Christmas after Willard and I were married was a strange one. Mother and Father had been terribly disappointed that I had married Willard. To them he was just a poor man, one far below my station in life." She swallowed and looked at her hands lying in her lap. "Mother and Father felt so strongly, they didn't have a lot to do with Willard and me the first few years of our marriage."

For a long while Mrs. Thurman sat thoughtfully, staring off but not really seeing anything in the here and now. "We had a tiny two-room apartment in Pittsburgh above Oscar Payton's garage. The only real furniture we had was a bed that Willard had purchased from a secondhand store. Everything else was boxes and crates that we arranged into a semblance of furniture." Mrs. Thurman laughed. This time there was genuine humor in her tone. "But Willard with his joking and carefree disposition made everything seem right. We had a small coal stove to keep us warm, but not very much coal. In the evenings, we'd let the stove burn down and then we'd climb into bed and bundle up in our blankets while I read aloud, or Willard would sing in his deep baritone, or we'd just talk and dream and plan the future. That's how we spent that first Christmas Eve, bundled up on our lumpy, secondhand bed trying to keep warm and having a marvelous time of it. I'd made a few decorations for the apartment, but everything was pretty bare. We each had one gift. Willard bought me a pair of wool socks so I wouldn't freeze my feet at night, and I bought him a pair of gloves. What an absolutely wonderful Christmas we had that year. I don't know that we ever went to sleep during that whole night. We read, played games, laughed, talked, and became terribly silly, but we were in love and nothing else seemed to matter."

Marge Thurman continued to stare off, the fond memory rushing back to her. "Willard was such a hard worker and so very, very brilliant that it wasn't very long before we were rather well-to-do. After that we had some very prosperous Christmases. But every Christmas Eve as we climbed into our great big, perfect bed we would talk about that first Christmas above Oscar Payton's garage when we didn't have anything. But . . ." Mrs. Thurman closed her eyes. "But yet that first Christmas," she whispered longingly, "we had everything. And Willard would jokingly suggest that we find that old apartment in Pittsburgh and spend Christmas there. He looked at me with that mischievous twinkle in his eyes and said, 'Margie, we're not getting any younger. If we don't go this year, we might never have a chance again.'" Her eyes filled with tears. "I should have taken him up on his wild offer," she whispered.

Mrs. Thurman wiped her eyes. "Well, it's getting late. I'd better get back and let you folks enjoy your Christmas Eve together."

I shuddered as I thought of Marge Thurman stepping out into the cold, black night, crossing the deserted street, marching up her silent driveway, and entering her big house only to rattle about in its bleak, lonely emptiness. It was as though my young heart melted inside me, and more than anything I longed to reach out and protect this old lady, this elderly neighbor whom I had rather despised not so many days previously. I was so ashamed of the horrible feelings that I had harbored against Mrs. Thurman. All those days my cold, covetous eyes had seen only a rich, self-ish woman stingily hoarding so much wealth in her huge home while I had nothing. Now I could see how terribly mistaken I had been. In the midst of my loving, caring family I had so very much more than poor Mrs. Thurman, wandering around in her big house by herself.

I don't exactly remember what motivated me next. All I remember is feeling an overwhelming sense of urgency to do something memorable for Marge Thurman, something that would help soothe the sting of this Christmas without Willard. Before I could even work things out clearly in my mind, I pushed up from the sofa and darted for the Christmas tree. Dropping to my knees and reaching beneath the pungent, prickly branches, I grabbed the soft, puffy package that was the Christmas quilt. Surreptitiously, I plucked the white card from its top and dropped it under the tree, and then, clutching the package to my breast while tears brimmed in my eyes, I turned back to Mrs. Thurman. "Before you go," I called out imploringly, "you have to take your Christmas present. It's one I made." I set the colorfully wrapped package in her lap.

"For me?" Mrs. Thurman gasped, looking at me while her hands ran uncertainly across the crinkled surface of the stiff wrapping paper. She seemed to hold her breath, waiting for my answer, and in that moment I realized that if God really intended me to be an answer to Mrs. Thurman's prayers, He had probably been preparing me long before this moment. He who knew everything, even my own selfish heart, had to have known that my quilt was destined for Mrs. Thurman.

"For you," I stammered. "It's yours. I made it especially . . ." I swallowed, suddenly choking on my teeming emotions while a flood of serene warmth washed through me, causing my heart to swell. "I think I made it especially for you. Wendy helped, and my friend Jennilynn, and my teacher from church. I hope you like it." I swallowed again, blinking back my tears. "Do you mind opening it here?" I asked. "So everybody can see it." I didn't dare look in Wendy's direction because I was sure she would think that I had completely lost my mind.

Staring down at the package in her lap, Mrs. Thurman savored the moment. Slowly her fingers groped about the edges of the paper and finally pulled back the wrapping. She gasped as soon as she saw the first colors of the quilt. Looking up at me and then down at the quilt, she tugged the paper back and slowly unfolded the giant quilt. "Oh, my, it's so beautiful," she whispered. "Absolutely gorgeous." She ran her hands gently across the quilt. "And it's so soft," she whispered wonderingly. "So very, very soft." She pressed it to her cheek and wrapped her arms around it. "This is a winter quilt," she stated in amazement. "The cold will never penetrate this."

Mrs. Thurman pushed the wrapping paper aside and clutched the quilt to her chest. Slowly she stood and wrapped its soft warmth about her. Sinking back onto the sofa with the quilt draped around her arms and shoulders, she laughed out loud. "Willard would have loved it. This is the kind of quilt we needed our first Christmas above Oscar Payton's garage." She snuggled soothingly inside the Christmas quilt and closed her eyes. "What a wonderful gift," she whispered. "It will always remind me of Willard." She swallowed, opened her eyes, and then added, glancing in my direction, "And of you. I won't be cold anymore. Every time I wrap up in this beautiful quilt, I'll remember this very special night. How did you ever know?" she rasped, choking back her emotions. "How could you possibly know to make me such a wonderful gift?"

I smiled, tears shimmering in my eyes while my emotions swelled to the point of bursting. "Actually," I confessed softly, "I really didn't know, but remember how you prayed?" I laughed softly. "Heavenly Father always hears a prayer. He knew. He knew what you needed, and He helped me discover how to make it for you."

"And I was beginning to wonder if God ever listened to my prayers. I'll have to pray more often, because He *must* know who I am."

I laughed. "And I guess He knows who I am, too," I exclaimed joyfully, my voice breaking. "If He didn't know me, how could He have counted on me to make your quilt?"

Mrs. Thurman reached out and clasped one of my hands between both of hers. "Thank you. Thank you so very much. What an absolutely marvelous Christmas this has been." She took in a deep breath. "But now I really must go and leave all of you to your Christmas festivities." Slowly she stood and began tenderly folding the quilt. When it was folded and she had put on her coat, she started toward the front door.

Just before Mrs. Thurman slipped into the night, she turned back to us, a worried look furrowing her brow. Holding up her free hand, she spoke reluctantly, "I know it's a lot to ask, perhaps more than I have a right to ask. I haven't been a very good neighbor. In fact, I've been a rather bad neighbor." She swallowed and pressed on. "I know you probably have everything planned for tomorrow, but perhaps you wouldn't mind terribly if . . ." She had a hard time getting the words out of her mouth. "Would you mind," she went on in a hoarse, weak voice, "coming to my house tomorrow for Christmas dinner?" Seeming to fear a hasty rejection, she quickly added, "I have all of that food and no one to eat it, but . . ." She closed her eyes for a brief moment, opened them, and burst out, "I would probably need help cooking the meal. It's been so very long since I cooked a Christmas dinner." She looked longingly at me. "Anyone who can make such a beautiful quilt can surely cook Christmas dinner." She turned hopefully to Mom. "Please, Mrs. Cluff."

The whole family sat in stunned silence. "You would like us to go to your house for Christmas dinner?" Mom stammered. "But there are so many of us."

"Yes," Mrs. Thurman rasped, her voice breaking as she clutched my quilt. "Please, will you come?"

"We could all help," Wendy spoke up, smiling.

Mom grinned broadly. "Well, I suppose Wendy is committed." I nodded my head furiously. Mom looked about the room at the rest of the family. They all shrugged and nodded.

As soon as Mrs. Thurman was gone, I turned to Mom and Dad and ventured softly, "I thought I had made the quilt for both of you." I swallowed. "But I couldn't let Mrs. Thurman go without giving her something." Tears filled my eyes and my voice broke. "I'll make you another one. I promise. And it will be even better than that one."

"Oh, sweet Nadine," Mom whispered, dabbing at her eyes with her fingertips, "it couldn't possibly be better than that one, because as soon as you gave it to Mrs. Thurman it became the most wonderful quilt ever."

Jennilynn called late Christmas Eve. As soon as I picked up the receiver, she burst out in a flood of excitement, "They loved it, Nadine. I couldn't wait till Christmas morning. I had to give Mom and Dad the quilt tonight. Of course, Mom bawled, and Dad sniffled and blubbered a little. Thanks for helping me make it. Did you give yours to your mom and dad?"

"Actually, I gave it to Marge Thurman," I explained gently.

"Marge Thurman!" Jennilynn practically screamed. "Why would you give your beautiful quilt to Marge Thurman? She's the very last person that deserves it."

"Maybe that's why I gave it to her," I answered softly. "I wanted her to have it."

There was a pause on the other end of the line. "Is that part of the giving thing?" Jennilynn questioned curiously.

I laughed. "I think that's the best part."

"Nadine," Jennilynn asked quietly, "I know that I've asked tons of favors from you, and you've always given them, but could I ask for one more?"

I laughed. "Jen, you're such a goof. What favors have you asked for?"

"This Christmas you let me be part of your giving thing, Nadine."

"Jen, it was never *my* giving thing. My mom started it, and she just borrowed it—from Jesus. He's the one that did the giving thing better than anyone. The rest of us just try to copy Him. And you copied Him so much better than I ever did."

"I knew you'd say something like that," Jennilynn returned quietly. She hesitated, cleared her throat, and then added, "And that's why I thought you might give me one more thing."

"Like what?"

"You know when we go back to school in January, everybody gets to tell what they got for Christmas?" Involuntarily I shuddered at the thought. It was that bit of sharing that had caused me to hide behind the giving thing in the first place. "Well, Nadine, will you let me be the one to tell everyone about the giving thing?" Then she quickly added, "I promise to tell them that it was all your idea. Please."

I laughed. "Of course, you can tell them, but like I told you, it was never my giving thing. At least, it wasn't until I finally figured it out."

* * *

We had a wonderful Christmas dinner with Mrs. Thurman. I had never seen so much food. And after that, Mrs. Thurman told us that her door was always open to us. In fact, she insisted that I visit her every day of the Christmas holiday. When I visited her the first time, she invited me in and served chocolate-frosted cookies on real china, and milk in a genuine crystal glass. As we sat on the giant sofa in her living room, Marge laid the Christmas quilt across our legs and laps. She spoke of her travels, of Willard, of her son and granddaughters, and of life in Eagar as well as her life before she ever visited the White Mountains of Arizona. I discovered her pent-up, sad loneliness and realized that her previous aura of arrogance was just a fear-induced mask. She was not at all aloof as I had once supposed, merely self-conscious, disoriented, and deprived of companionship.

The Sunday before returning to school, I awoke with a fever, my throat burning and my whole body aching. I felt horrible and instinctively knew that I was going to feel just as bad or worse the next morning when it was time to return to school.

"Do you know what I think?" Mom mused as she touched my forehead with the back of her hand and caressed my cheek and forehead. "I think there is one young lady in this house who is going to have an extended holiday. You've got yourself a full-blown case of the flu."

"The flu?" I gasped painfully.

"I'm sure of it." Mom sighed and shook her head.

For a moment I contemplated the strange irony; last year I would have loved to miss the first day back to school after Christmas. I burst out laughing, even though it hurt my throat.

"And what's so funny about being sick?" Mom inquired, perplexed.

I shook my head, closed my eyes, and smiled. "I guess the flu is one of my Christmas gifts, one I hadn't counted on." I laughed and shrugged. "And this year I didn't even need it."

Mom touched my forehead again. "Whatever are you talking about?"

I smiled, shook my head knowingly, and reflected happily on the giving thing.

ALMA J. YATES

About the Author

Alma J. Yates was born in Brigham City, Utah, and raised on a small farm just outside of town. From 1970 to 1972, he served as an LDS missionary in the West Mexico Mission. Later he attended Weber State College and BYU, graduating from BYU with a major in English and later with a master's degree in educational administration. After teaching English for seven years, he moved into school administration. Currently he is the principal of Highland Primary School in Snowflake, Arizona.

Alma began writing professionally while he was attending BYU. Since that time he has published several articles and short stories in the Church magazines, as well as published several short-story collections and almost a dozen novels. He is married to Margery Nadine "Nicki" Cluff, and they are the parents of seven sons and one daughter.